"MYSTICAL ...OGY"

RETRIBUTION

RETRIBUTION

Enjoy the story
Alan Principal

Alan Principal

© Alan Principal, 2014

Published by Alan Principal

Intellectual Property & Copyright © Alan Principal 2011

First paperback edition printed 2014 in the United Kingdom

All rights reserved. No part of this book may be reproduced, adapted, stored in a retrieval system or transmitted by any means, electronic, mechanical, photocopying, or otherwise without the prior written permission of the author.

The rights of Alan Principal to be identified as the author of this work have been asserted in accordance with the Copyright, Designs and Patents Act 1988.

This novel is a work of fiction. Names and characters are the product of the author's imagination or historical facts or folklore used with no offensive or slanderous intent. The publisher and author assume no responsibility for errors or omission from the date of printing.

A CIP catalogue record for this book is available from the British Library.

ISBN 978-0-9930139-1-1

Book layout and cover design by Clare Brayshaw

Cover image © Konradbak | Dreamstime.com

Prepared, printed and distributed by:

York Publishing Services Ltd
64 Hallfield Road
Layerthorpe
York YO31 7ZQ

Tel: 01904 431213

Website: www.yps-publishing.co.uk

About the author

Alan is a proud Yorkshireman. He was born, brought up and educated in Doncaster where he still lives with his loving wife Sylvia. His ability as a creative writer was completely missed by his teacher, who wrongly and severely punished him. His 'crime' (for homework at the age of 10) – writing a beautiful poem about the harvest. She thought he'd copied it from a book. Sadly  he didn't resume creatively using his pen until he finished his 3 year service in the Aerial Photo Intelligence section of the Royal Air Force.

His work roles, which eventually steered him to some serious yet pleasant writing, have included teaching and helping thousands of people to drive, training, lecturing, features in the local press, FE teaching, submission writing and a wide range of vocational programme guides for NVQ's to level 4. In 1991 he almost managed to attract the Royal Armouries to a Doncaster site.

Since virtually retiring, he has enjoyed writing quizzes for the company he set up in 1994. In his role as Quizmaster he uses his birth name as he did in his previous involvements.

During the last few years, he has enjoyed writing a kaleidoscope of poetry of both serious and humorous rhymes – a book will probably surface in 2015.

But his greatest authorial love has been penning a series of four exciting and mystical, gripping action packed 'crossover' adventure stories, particularly suitable for those aged 10-20 but good armchair or bedtime reading for all family members who are 'young at heart' aged 10 to 100.

The twins featured with their parents in the first of the four captivating stories 'The Twins Destiny Begins' are 15 years old. In book 2 – 'Retribution' they reach 17, and are 20 in the third and fourth of the sequential stories.

Dedication

I dedicate this book to my wonderful and loving wife Sylvia, without whom the story would never have been told.

My grateful thanks also go to our good friend Patsy Daniels, who helped with the editing and the first proof reading.

Thank you Ladies.

Alan

The Magpies Poem

One for sorrow
Two for joy
Three for a girl
Four for a boy
Five for silver
Six for gold
Seven, a second story now being told!

Contents

1	The Second Story Unfolds	1
2	A Knife Attack	9
3	Gemini Cave	19
4	Glistening Calcite Cavern	30
5	Observed Arrival	40
6	Merlin Deceived & Imprisoned	51
7	Laybent Castle Dungeon	57
8	The Great Escape	68
9	A Perfect End to a Day	78
10	Moatcaster Castle Re-Visited	91
11	Merlin's Invisible Crystal Tower	99
12	Buzzed On the Beach	107
13	A Swarm of Stingers	112
14	Alien Abductions	117
15	'They Can Fly As Well'	123
16	Suspended Animation	131
17	Trouble in Cliffthorpe Bay	140
18	Fun That Went Wrong	147

19	A Huge Shadow Appeared	156
20	Medieval Jousting Discussed	162
21	The Twins Lose Their Powers	169
22	The Knights Fight Each Other	173
23	The Main and Final Event	183

Chapter One

THE SECOND STORY UNFOLDS

Having quickly run downstairs, David met his twin sister Mary as they both entered the hall, just as she was en route to join him upstairs. Mary was closely followed by their parents, Sylvia and Bill, who had wondered why their daughter had so suddenly jumped up and rushed out of the room.

As the twins met, they grabbed each other's hands and turning towards their parents Mary excitedly exclaimed, 'They're here, there's something here! There's some sort of entity, a goblin or something somewhere outside!'

David went on to say, 'We both sensed it. We both felt them, or him or it or whatever it is, at the same time! But whatever it is, there most certainly is some sort of unwelcome "being" nearby, somewhere outside our house.'

'Yes,' Mary said, 'we had both become aware there was something outside that shouldn't be here, but why here and why now outside our home in Oxtown?'

'It's ages since we had anything to do with any sort of entities or creatures from the Other Side,' David said, 'but there is definitely at least one. There is some sort of unwelcome being somewhere close to the house.'

'But why, David,' Mary repeated herself, 'why are they or it here at all? There has to be a good reason, a very good reason.'

At that point, Bill started to lead everyone back into the lounge, suggesting they all take a seat and try to relax for a minute while they talked things through. So they settled down onto their dark green leather suite.

'It could possibly be something to do with our Castershire holiday next week,' Bill said. 'It's two years or just a little over since we were last there, when we had that awesome supernatural battle and you were successful in defeating and killing King Offalmire.'

'And Merlin and the Terrestrial Light Gods were so pleased with you,' Sylvia added.

'But your mum and I,' Bill said, 'had both been aware of what had been planned for you on that trip, as we had known for years about the mythological destiny created for you centuries ago, by the Gods of the Terrestrial Light. We also knew you were to become the Terrestrial Twins in the supernatural midnight ceremony on your fifteenth birthday.

'Your mum and I had also known long before the pair of you were born, that both of you were going to be blessed with awesome supernatural powers. Mind blowing abilities, far greater than those of any normal human being, in that amazing and what also proved to be such an unforgettably eventful ceremony. But I can assure you twins, we know absolutely nothing of any events to coincide with this next trip, the start of our holiday in Castershire next week, honest! Or we certainly would have talked to you about it.

'You're seventeen now, and having become the Terrestrial Twins, with who knows how many exceptional abilities, why on earth would we even attempt to keep either of you in the dark about anything? It would be pointless, as you would probably be more than capable of dealing with any problems or events that cropped up, whatever they were!'

The twins had been born on the night of the Summer Solstice for magical reasons, to enable them to fulfill their mythological destiny. Their particular hair colours, for the same sort of supernatural reasons, are the same as their parents. Mary's being ash blonde and almost white like her mother's. David's the opposite, as black as a raven, just like his father's.

The colours black and white, when magically linked, are just one of a number of significantly important factors which help make up crucial parts of a special mythological plan. The combination of factors that collided in their birth eventually enabled Mary and David to become the supernaturally and awesomely powered Terrestrial Twins, earthly envoys of the Terrestrial Light Gods having being created and blessed by the gods to assist them in their responsibilities as protectors of all Earthly beings, mainly human beings, from any warped powers or evil, criminal individuals.

The first task for David and Mary in their new supernatural role, following the blessing ceremony by the Terrestrial Light Gods when they were endowed with monumental powers, had been the enormously difficult and extremely dangerous task of ridding the world of King Offalmire, the evil master of the Other World. This task they admirably achieved and Offalmire had melted down to a pile of disgusting bubbling mucus before being totally removed, leaving a stained patch on the lawn outside the King's Tower in Moatcaster Castle.

The twins are physical images of their parents. David is an athletic young man who looks just like his father, Bill. Mary is the image of their attractive mother, Sylvia, who amazingly has Merlin in her family tree. Both their parents were born and had lived in Castershire, where they met. The ancestors of both their families had also lived in the same region for centuries and had been White Witches, but no longer practiced the art.

'Your dad is right,' Sylvia said, 'we haven't got a clue as to why we should have any kind of entity prowling around our house and I wish they or it weren't here at all, whatever the reason.

'Two years ago, as a remarkable team, we were able to get rid of that evil and obnoxious King Offalmire, and so prevented him from getting at the supernatural Thirteen Treasures of Britain. As we know, Merlin had hidden them in the invisible crystal tower which he so cleverly concealed inside Moatcaster Castle's King's Tower. But as your clever strategies got rid of Offalmire, he not only didn't get at the Treasures, but he's no longer any sort of problem either.

'So,' continued Sylvia, 'as Offalmire has been dead for two years and the magical Thirteen Treasures are still hidden and safe, why, as Mary has said, have we got unwelcome visitors at all and why now?'

'If you and Mum don't know why they're here, Dad,' David said, 'and both sis and I can assure you they are out there, there definitely is some sort of being giving off a negative energy outside our house...

'Hang on a minute though!' David suddenly exclaimed. 'Mary and I are both suddenly sensing something. There is something happening somewhere that isn't right. We have just received a substantial feeling that an event has occurred or is being planned to take place that is of major importance.

'And as we all know from our past experiences, the only reason they are here is because our very existence is a threat to somebody or something that has negative energies, particularly those used against human beings. And whoever or whatever it is, that "being", or more to the point whoever sent it, would very much like to see both me and Sis and possibly, I'm sorry, Mum, all of us…dead.'

'Yes,' Mary said agreeing with David, 'it's got to be something very important for them to be here at all and it's because of something that's in the process of happening, or which has recently occurred. More strangely, it is an event of which none of us are even remotely aware! I also find it odd that Merlin has not been in touch with us either. Surely he would be the one to know what it is that is happening, or is planned. He's always informed us in the past.

David then continued, 'We don't need to worry too much about what is outside though. Whatever it is, it can't get in to us. We still have the safety shield in place which we created round the house.'

'Thanks for that, Son,' Bill said with a little relief in his voice, 'but it still doesn't answer the question as to why they're here? Let's just sit quietly for a minute or two and see if we can come up with an answer, just in case we have forgotten anything.'

With that, and with tense expressions on all their faces, the four Knight family members sat back in deep thought to search their minds.

Sylvia was the first one to break the silence. 'A little over two years ago we all witnessed Offalmire shrivel up and die. Yes!'

David butted in with, 'And Merlin thanked us for doing such a monumental favour for mankind in such a competent manner.'

'Yes, we know all that,' Bill said, sounding a little agitated, 'but that doesn't give us an answer for what is happening now.' But after a brief pause he went on to say, 'Or does it?'

That gave them all cause to sit back again in silent thought.

Then, and for a reason best known only to himself, David surprised everyone by asking, 'Were there any goblins, or any sort of entities around here when we were due to be born, Mum?'

'Yes,' Sylvia replied, 'your dad saw at least one drift across the lawn, just as we were leaving for the hospital.'

'And I told you about our nightmare journey,' Bill said, 'and also the creatures in the hospital.'

Mary then picked up on the conversation, 'So if that all happened seventeen years ago, having goblins or something else around our house now means an event just as big or possibly as important is occurring, or is being planned, and they don't want any of us to prevent it from happening.'

'But we know that, Sis,' David said. 'What we want in fact what we need, to know is what the actual event is and the reason behind them or it being here. They are obviously aware we are going to Castershire on holiday next week and must think that one of the reasons we are going is to try to prevent whatever it is from taking place.'

'We're being seen as a ruddy threat again, aren't we?' Mary said, somewhat annoyed. 'Why can't they just leave us alone?'

'It's because you're the Terrestrial Twins, love,' Bill said sympathetically, 'you will always be seen as a major threat by any beings from the Other World, who or whatever they are, because of who and what you two have become. And we all know there are only two things in our world that any of us can do about it... nothing and fizz-all! But it has been two years since you were last threatened, so I suppose as Terrestrial Twins special activities go, it's not too bad really.'

'Dad's right, Sis. Whether we like it or not we became an extraordinarily special set of twins. We are no longer just ordinary people. But we've managed to live normal lives for the last two years without any problems and have learned to accept that the supernatural powers, abilities and wisdom we have been blessed with are going to be with us for a long, long time. And if and whenever we are needed by the Terrestrial Light Gods we will do what is required of us.'

Mary then joined in with, 'I know you have accepted what has happened to us a bit more easily than I have, Bruv. I realize we both have enormous responsibilities in our special role as protectors of terrestrial beings, particularly human beings. However, I feel I have only recently come to grips with accepting who and what we are. Like you, David, I have finally realized our incredible abilities are a blessing and not a curse, and have accepted what they are and how best we might use them. I have also come to realize that having such powers helps us to cope and deal with whatever it is that comes our way and have helped me when I had doubts.'

'Anyway, Mary,' David said to lighten the conversation, 'you were saying only last week that you had discovered some new things and experiences about yourself that you were enjoying, so why complain now?'

Mary, looking a little embarrassed, indignantly replied, 'I don't know what you're talking about. Anyway, I spoke to you in confidence after you told me something about yourself that I still find hard to believe!'

'That will do, that's enough,' their mum butted in. 'You're getting too old to sound like little children, so let's get back to focusing all our thoughts on our unwelcome visitors to see if we can find a solution or reason for them being here.'

'How's this for a thought then,' David said in an excited voice, 'Offalmire is dead! So who the hell is it that we are possibly posing a threat to now?'

There was silence for a second or two while everyone pondered on David's monumental remark.

This time it was Mary that broke the silence. She reached out to grasp David's hands in a twinning hold and said tensely, 'I know we have talked about it generally, but do you think there really is someone else somewhere out there who we also might have to kill, or worse, who really is trying to kill us?'

Chapter Two

A KNIFE ATTACK

Again there was silence in the room, as no one really knew what to say. It was Sylvia who finally spoke, and she was obviously upset. 'My God, Bill! If the twins are right, and it now seems they might be, we're all in danger again. But why? We haven't heard a thing as to what it might be all about. What I really don't understand is, and I know I said it earlier, why have we not heard from Merlin?'

Bill went over to sit on the arm of his wife's chair and took hold of her hand. 'Steady on, love, we don't know anything at the moment so we must stay calm. Winding ourselves up will not do us any good at all. The entity or whatever it is the twins sensed might just have been passing, going on to somewhere else. We really don't know yet what to think. For all we know they might just be fairies at the bottom of the garden!' And he squeezed her hand. 'So until we do know a bit more about what is happening, love, let's all just try to keep calm. We'll learn nothing by winding ourselves up.'

'Thanks for that, love. And you're right,' Sylvia replied, 'but I think the twins by now know the difference between fairies and entities.'

'Dad's got a point though, Mum,' David said, 'we haven't seen them yet even though Sis and I have sensed their unwelcome presence outside. As it or they haven't as yet attempted to do anything, they might not be a threat. We'll just have to be on our guard.'

'I prefer to think they might be a problem,' Mary said, 'that way I can stay more alert and focused. And no matter what you and Dad think, David, I'm with Mum on this, we still feel threatened.'

'Can you two contact Merlin?' Bill asked. 'Or won't your telepathy reach that far?'

'That's a great idea, love,' Sylvia said with a little excitement in her voice. 'It's worth trying, kids. Isn't it?'

'Its funny that Dad's suggested it, because it's what both Sis and I have already mentally communicated with each other and were about to suggest we try! Our thoughts must have reached you too, Dad.'

Mary then took hold of David's hands and they again gripped each other to enable them to 'twin' together and so create an extremely powerful energy.

'Okay,' David said, 'let's do it, let's get rid of the unknown. It's that kind of stuff that spooks all of us. Here we go. We'll try to reach Merlin.'

With faces completely void of expression, the twins linked their minds in a combined effort to enable them to use some of their ever growing and incredible range of powers to form a unique mental telecommunications linking process in an attempt to reach Merlin.

Merlin had been deeply involved in most of their exploits two years ago when David and Mary became the Terrestrial Twins, and had been an unseen observer ready to support them when they needed it. He had also provided seven magical magpies for support, and as additional guardians and advisers. If anyone would know what was going on, it would be Merlin.

Bill gripped his wife's hand a little tighter when the expressions on the twins' faces turned firstly to one of surprise, then to one of amazed disbelief as they relaxed their twinning hold to sit back.

'That's unbelievable!' David blurted out. 'Ruddy unbelievable!'

But before their parents could say anything, Mary, as astonished as David, butted in saying, 'David's absolutely right. It really is unbelievable and I would have forgiven him if he had properly sworn.'

'But why?' Bill asked, now with some shock in his voice, 'Why? What is it for goodness sake?'

Their mum came in at this point sounding even more stressed. 'What is it, twins, what's happened or what is happening?'

'We did it,' David said in a surprised yet pleased voice. 'We formed a telecommunications mind link with Merlin, but the big surprise and shock is.....Offalmire had a son! He's got a ruddy son!'

'Yes,' Mary said, in a more subdued voice. 'Apparently he witnessed all of the Moatcaster Castle battle in which we killed his father King Offalmire in that awesome scrap. But seemingly, the weird thing is, before Offalmire's gooey remains were cleared away by Merlin, his son magically penetrated the ground under the slimy sludge and absorbed much of his father's powers, or whatever there was left of them.'

David then continued with the story. 'And now, at the age of twenty, he has almost enough power to get into the Crystal Tower and get at the Thirteen Treasures.'

'And that's why there's a goblin here,' Mary said. Somewhat to their relief, she and David had established that the presence outside was attributable to only one skulking emissary. 'Well,' she continued, 'at least there's only one right now. Offalmire's son is obviously looking for ways to prevent us from stopping him.'

'That really is a weird story,' their mum said, 'does it or he have a name, or do we just have to refer to him as him?'

Their mum's comment put the first proper smile on everyone's face, which was a pleasant relief from what they had been experiencing over the last few minutes.

'We don't know, Mum,' David replied, 'but Merlin said we would all have to be very careful, and that he would contact us when we arrive in Castershire.'

'So again, we are a threat,' Mary said, anger showing in her voice, 'and so is he or it!' She then after a slight pause more calmly said, 'But now we most certainly are a very real threat to him. We are now two years older and wiser, and much, much more capable physically, mentally and supernaturally than we were last time. Then we had only just been blessed with our powers but since then they have continued growing more powerful and more comprehensive. Who or whatever he is, he'd better watch out. Somehow I don't feel as threatened any more.' The strain which had been showing in her face had been replaced by a much happier broad smile.

'Well said, Sis!' David said. 'And we obviously learned a lot about developing strategies and planning in our fight against Offalmire,' he added with an air of confidence. 'So if there's to be a fight, we'll be ready for it and very capable of winning.'

Sylvia still looked puzzled. 'But I wonder why Merlin didn't let us know what was happening?' she asked again. 'Perhaps we could have done something about it.'

'I don't think so, Mum,' David replied, 'I don't think we could have done anything at all, and we certainly can't do anything now until we get to Castershire.'

'It does seem strange,' agreed Mary. 'Merlin knew about Offalmire's son but it seems that's as much as he did know. I am absolutely sure he would have contacted us if he thought it necessary.'

'I think you're right, love,' Bill agreed, 'we'll just have to wait and see. It's Wednesday today and we're leaving on Saturday morning, so it won't be long before we know the facts and details. We will then be able to work out what, if anything, we can or need to do about it.

'In the meantime your mum and I have got martial arts classes booked which we have to deliver tonight and tomorrow night. We were also hoping you two would be free to give our groups a couple of demonstrations.' Bill looked expectantly at the twins. 'You know how much the members appreciate them, particularly the younger ones. With you two still being teenagers and having such high fighting skills, plus the fact that both of you have achieved black belts and second Dan, there's no doubt they all look up to both of you. You truly are shining examples of what we teach and stand for.

'Of course they don't realize it is your Terrestrial Twins powers that have been added to your previously achieved abilities and skill levels that help you to achieve such high standards and allow you to deliver such awesome demonstrations. And they can't understand why you no longer compete. But we agreed it was a small price to pay, particularly as you can use your combined skills and abilities to show off some of the skills it might be possible for them to achieve. They all really do love both of you for it.'

'You're on, Dad,' David said, 'we realized you were going to ask us anyway, so Sis and I had already agreed we would. You know how much we love doing it.'

'You don't read our minds all the time, do you?' their mum asked, a note of trepidation in her voice.

David jokingly replied, 'All the time, Mum!'

'Now stop teasing your mum, David,' Bill said, 'I don't want her worrying all day about it.'

'Sorry, Mum, I was only joking, honest.'

'Meantime,' Bill said, a serious tone in his voice, 'we have got to be on guard against any problems. We must stay alert and make sure we all stay alive. Four of us are going on holiday on Saturday and I would like to think there will be four of us coming back.'

They all looked a bit grim following Bill's last remark, but realized he was absolutely right. 'Carelessness costs lives is an old phrase but it is still a true one.'

'Will we all be wearing our favourite Seven Magpies black strip?' Mary asked, turning to her mum.

'Yes, love, we will. I've made sure we've got plenty of spare sets as well, including caps and a couple of spare bum-bags just in case we need them. They were the first things I got ready for the suitcases, and there are sets for everybody to wear when we travel on Saturday. You know how proud your dad and I are of our Seven Magpies Martial Arts Studio and its logo! You both learned how important the seven magical magpies are to all of us from our adventurous experiences two years ago. And you know why we included them in our business name and logo. There is no way we would go on holiday without our magpies strip. We're always proud to show-off our logo as we know you two are and do, which is particularly good as our martial arts involvements are not only a great hobby but are our business. A business in which you two will become partners next year on your eighteenth birthdays!' The twins just grinned.

'Will we be stopping in Forest Valley again?' Mary asked. 'We might see that old lady who looked like a witch if we do.'

'I don't see why not,' replied Bill, 'but we've got to be on our guard wherever we go.' Then turning to his wife he continued, 'What do you think, love?'

'I think you're right, Bill. We're a threat or a target wherever we are, or whatever we try to do, so stopping for a meal again en route doesn't really make any difference. Yes, love, it's okay with me.'

'I wouldn't mind trying to catch something in that lake we had a problem with last time,' David said, 'perhaps I'll have a little more luck this time.'

'In that case,' Sylvia said, 'Mary and I can have that bike ride in the forest. It didn't quite work out for us last time either, did it? So like you and your dad, David, perhaps we all can try again.'

'Right, David,' Bill said getting up from his chair, 'in that case, we'll go into the garage and check out all the fishing gear and wipe down and oil all of the bikes just to spruce them up a bit. We don't want to be putting grubby bikes into our new car, do we? I'd also like to show you the new Seven Magpies logos we had fitted on both of the car's front doors, David, it looks really smart!'

'And I suppose you two will be wanting to do a bit of driving now you've both passed your driving tests this week?' their mum said. 'You weren't satisfied with just passing your motorcycle tests last week were you?' The twins just smiled.

'Well, if you two are going to the garage,' Sylvia said, 'Mary can help me with a bit of the packing and writing a shopping list for some of the things we will need to take with us. We can then pick them up later or even tomorrow. But I don't want to leave the supermarket trip until Friday.'

Once out of the house and away from the girls, Bill voiced his concerns to David about the new threat they were experiencing.

'I am really sorry, Son,' he said, 'but it appears you and your sister won't be able to enjoy a proper holiday like other young adults. We couldn't do anything about you both becoming the Terrestrial Twins as that was the main part of your destiny, and you did an excellent job by ridding the world of Offalmire two years ago. But it does seem a bit unfair that you probably have to take on another evil being and some of his helpers again.'

'Don't worry about it, Dad. Mary and I realize our responsibilities. It's part and parcel of the job of who and what we have become. We also realize, as we said back in the house, we are now two years older and our special supernatural powers and abilities have certainly grown with us. You won't be aware of it, but the range and strength of our abilities have definitely improved and become even more powerful. I don't think I would be exaggerating if I said some were now really awesome. You don't need to worry about me and Sis, we'll be fine.'

'Thanks for that, Son. I think I will be able to feel a lot happier now.'

Shortly after they had laid the folding bikes down outside the garage ready for a once-over and oiling, David spotted the unwelcome visitor they had sensed earlier and whispered to his dad.

'There's an unwelcome guest in the garden behind the rhododendron bush at the side of the drive. I would say he looks more like an elf than a goblin and he's wearing a brown hoodie. Let's lean this old mirror at an angle against the garage bench, that way I'll be able to watch him in it when I turn my back to him.'

Bill then helped his son to position the mirror and David knelt down facing the garage, supposedly checking a bike but keeping an eye on the mirror. He was now ready for anything...

Barely half a minute had passed before David spotted the entity rushing up behind him brandishing a knife he obviously meant to use in an attempt to kill him.

Just before it reached him, David performed a smart rolling dive to his left and his strong well-aimed side kick knocked the wind out of the surprised elf, and also diverted his lunging attack sideways. Bill, who was also ready for him, then gave him a really nasty crack on the back of the head with a heavy spanner. David followed up by zapping him with a sizzling blue flash, and that was that. It was all over in seconds.

They picked up its lifeless body between them and took it round the house to the bottom of the garden where it was unceremoniously dumped onto the rubbish heap. They then had a closer look at it.

'It looks different to the things we saw two years ago,' Bill said. 'If anything it's uglier with a more piggish face and a muddy sort of texture to its skin. I was also surprised that it didn't instantly become a pile of messy clothes when you zapped it like the other entities did last time.'

'Yes, that is a bit odd,' David replied, 'so I'd better get rid of it.' Pointing his forefinger at it, he then shot out an electric bolt of blue shimmering light. The creature then bubbled down to the usual pool of slimy mucus which they had become so accustomed to seeing two years ago.

On the way back to the garage David said, 'Well that's one down, Dad, and thankfully I don't sense any more. But I wonder how many more might there be that we will need to get rid of before we are done? You know Mary and I aren't happy when we have to do the things we find ourselves having to do. However, we have the responsibility that comes with our role as the Terrestrial Twins, so we do what we have to do. We also realize it's either us or them, so it has to be them.'

'Let's just hope there will be no more unwelcome beings of any sort here today, and hopefully not too many more when we go away. Our experiences two years ago and the volume of times we all found ourselves literally fighting for our lives, was more than enough. I am sure we can live without repeating that.'

'We'll tell Mum and Mary that....the elf has left the building!'

Chapter Three

GEMINI CAVE

It was a hot and sunny day similar to the start of their previous Castershire holiday two years earlier. But this time their two week holiday started near the end of July rather than June to allow the twins to take their driving and motorcycle tests, following their seventeenth birthdays.

The traffic hadn't been too bad and the journey had fortunately been uneventful, apart from one incident on a roundabout involving a motorcyclist dressed in a brown one-piece suit. His head was totally covered by a brown helmet which was fitted with a full face visor, making it impossible to see his face. He had done his best to try and force their car off the road, but David had come to the rescue by flattening his rear tyre with a well-aimed zap. The last they saw of him was accompanying his motorbike as it slammed into a hawthorn hedge and disappeared. Having left him behind, they continued on their journey towards Forest Valley where they had planned to stop for lunch.

'You've parked the car in exactly the same spot as you did last time, Dad!' David said when they stopped in the café's car park.

'Yes, Mary added, 'but is it a coincidence, or is there another reason for it?'

'I think it's just coincidence,' their mum said as they walked away from their car. Then she turned back to admiringly look at their car and remarked, 'I've always liked our Seven Magpies logos on the car doors. They look really smart against the black.'

Mary then butted in. 'As we've stopped at the same café as last time for lunch, we might see that old lady again who looked like a witch. I tried talking to you on Wednesday about her when we were packing, Mum, but your thoughts seemed miles away and you didn't answer me.'

'Yes, I'm sorry, love, I was thinking about all sorts of things, particularly about you and your brother again being threatened. It's something that parents have difficulty in accepting or can easily dismiss, even if you are the Terrestrial Twins. Your dad and I realize you two are much more capable nowadays, but you are still our children.'

'I know, Mum,' Mary replied, 'we realize it's not your choice any more than it was ours. But you know we had no say in the matter, it was and is our destiny. And as David has said, we are who and what we are, and as much as it won't always be easy we have fully accepted what we have become.'

David joined in the conversation at this point, 'There's no need to worry, Mum, really. We'll be fine! We know we have again been threatened, but it doesn't worry us so much. Plus, we can't afford to let it worry us or we could possibly end up in a fight feeling we might not win, and that would never do. Losing is not an option!'

Bill diplomatically interrupted, 'Well we're here at the café, and as we are ready to eat I suggest we go in and do just that.'

'And who knows,' Sylvia said, 'perhaps we might see that witch-looking old lady again. I know you two would love that.'

As much as they had spoken a number of times about the possibility of seeing the old lady, they were still very surprised when, as they walked into the café, there she was. The witch looking woman was sitting at the same table in the same chair as she had been two years earlier when they first saw her, as though she was a permanent fixture. No one said a word until they were seated on the same chairs and at the same table as last time.

Oddly enough it was Sylvia who spoke first. 'I don't know about the rest of you, but I most certainly am experiencing a strong and weird feeling that everything we're currently doing we have done before.'

'I think the rest of us feel the same way too, love,' Bill said, 'I believe it's referred to as déjà vu. It's as though we've turned the clock back two years and are now experiencing the same things for the first time, rather than for the second.'

'Not quite the same,' David added, 'last time we were here Mary and Mum went to the loo before they sat down. It was when they were coming back that they first saw the old lady, so she can't have been sitting there when you went to the loo last time or you would have seen her then? She must have materialized while you were in there and Dad and I didn't notice her arrival.'

'And we'll go first this time,' Mary said, then paused, 'and would you believe the old lady is actually smiling at us.'

'I can easily understand that,' David said jokingly.

'Don't start, you two,' Bill said, 'we can do without you two winding each other up.'

Bill then suggested he and David should see if she would smile at them when they went to the loo after the ladies had returned, and she did.

'She did smile at you two as well didn't she, Dad,' Mary said, 'or perhaps she fancies David,' she impishly said.

'Please, no more, you two or I'll have to set your mother on you,' Bill joked.

'Why bring me into it?' their mum asked, entering the spirit of the conversation. 'I personally think she thought all three of you were funny.' She then changed the subject asking, 'Sausage, mash and peas all right again for everybody?'

There was a rousing, 'Yes please,' from the three of them.

'But David isn't having an extra portion of peas this time, Mum, is he? Mary said. 'I know he's not a boy anymore, but he sometimes feels he has to act like one.'

'What's got into you two today?' Bill asked. 'You're beginning to annoy me, so stop it. Please don't spoil the start of our holiday.'

Sylvia then made an unusual remark. 'I've noticed that every time the twins wind each other up, the old lady has a little giggle to herself. You and David can't see her, Bill, but I can, and she's definitely happy when the twins are at each other. I think she is making them do it and she is shortening your tolerance level too, Bill.'

'I think you're right, Mum,' Mary said. 'David and I normally get on very well together, but we've both been a bit snidy since we came in. Sorry, Bruv.'

'No problem, Sis, if I feel like saying something sarcastic, I'll wait 'till we're outside again,' he said jokingly.

'But you know you were a bit disgusting in the car, David, on our last trip.'

'Let's try and forget what happened on our last trip,' Sylvia said.

'Now that is something I doubt any of us are going to be able to do, Mum,' David said, 'but we know what you mean.'

Bill then said, 'That's it, none of us are behaving as we normally would, so I suggest we get out of here before we place our order and find somewhere else for lunch, before we all fall foul of the spell that's obviously being cast our way.' And with that, he got up and shepherded his family out, leaving the waitress who was approaching their table with her order pad in her hand with a puzzled look. Bill, having shrugged his shoulders politely said, 'Sorry.' The old lady looked annoyed.

It didn't take them long to find another suitable café and they left straight after lunch, as the twins were again experiencing attempts by someone to telepathically contact them.

Once back in the relative safety of their car, they twinned, gripping hands and focused their minds on the signals they were receiving. David had the idea to use the speakers in the car's sound system to enable everyone to hear what was being said and to the delight of everybody it worked. Although Merlin's voice somehow sounded a bit different, it came through in stereo!

'I am most sorry, not only to have to interrupt your holiday plans, but also once more to put your lives in danger. The fact is, you the Terrestrial Twins with your parents' help, are the only combined powers strong enough and capable enough to be able to defeat and, if we have to, kill Offalmire's evil son.'

'Two years ago you did, and I use David's word, did such a brillfanmagically successful job ridding the world of the threat from King Offalmire.' They all smiled at his use of the word David had invented.

'Does Offalmire's son have a name?' David asked.

'Yes, he is called Drossmire,' Merlin replied. 'And from what I know of him, which is very little as he usually has a particularly powerful barrier round his little world, but what I can tell you is that he is as evil, if not more so, than his obnoxious father ever was!

'The supernatural Thirteen Treasures of Britain are again being threatened. Drossmire has to be stopped at all costs. Then, as you so expertly did with his father, he too will have to be removed. As I said earlier, I am most sorry to have to inflict this huge responsibility on you, but there is no one else, no individual or group capable of achieving what needs to be done.'

The short silence that followed Merlin's words seemed to last for ages, but was probably no more than five seconds. It was broken by Bill. 'Do you have a plan for removing Drossmire, Merlin, and what else is it you want the twins to do, and how do you propose we go about it?'

'Sadly I have to be honest with you all, Bill, at this juncture in time I have no idea what it is that Drossmire is planning, therefore I am not able to plan anything myself and so at present I am unable to guide you. What I do know is…..he appears to spend most of his time underground and in caves. That was why it was so easy for him to absorb his father's powers from beneath the dying sludge you had turned Offalmire into at the end of that incredible fight at Moatcaster Castle.

'He frequently time-ports himself from place to place and also from one cave to another, and at times enlists the help of cave dwelling entities to assist him and his goblin entourage. All that, plus the powers he absorbed from his father's sludge and the ability to shape-shift, makes him a very dangerous and formidable adversary.

'Messages I received from the Gods of the Terrestrial Light informed me he has recently been active in a number of caves, mainly in Castershire. However, his most recent trips have taken him to Gemini Cave which is only a short distance from where you are now in Forest Valley. Perhaps as you are so close, a visit may prove to be worthwhile.'

'Your dad and I were on our way to visit that very cave years ago,' Sylvia said, 'but a violent thunderstorm put us off. I for one wouldn't mind going to have a look at it, threat or no threat. I remember the poetry phrase written about it – *Neath a green leaf's mantle like sail in the forest and valley's green dale.*'

The car's sound system speakers quietened at this point as the unnatural voice of Merlin faded. He was gone.

'Can we go to Gemini Cave then, Dad?' Mary asked. 'It's ages since we were underground anywhere!'

'I don't see why not,' Bill replied, 'but we'll need to be extremely careful. We've no idea why Drossmire was there, but I am sure as a group, a magpie team, we'll be okay.'

'He may have been preparing a plan against us, possibly even a trap,' David said, 'but as he didn't know what we were going to be doing or where we were going, it should be all right. And who knows, we might even learn a thing or two that might be useful.'

'Okay,' Bill said, 'it seems we all want to go, so Gemini Cave it is. We'll have to forego the fishing trip and the bike ride though. We just won't have time to do everything.' He then programmed his sat-nav system and off they went.

They were all rather taken aback as they left the car park, and each of them experienced a feeling of trepidation. For standing next to the exit was the witch like old lady from the original café. She stood watching them, a macabre grin on her face.

'And what was that all about,' groaned Mary as they drove away.

'I have no idea, love,' replied Bill. 'I sincerely hope she's not going to follow us everywhere.'

A hundred yards up the road, David began chuckling to himself and remarked. 'I bet that witch woman isn't a twin.'

'I've a feeling I'm going to regret this,' his mum commented, 'but why do you think she's not a twin, Son?'

'Well...' David amusingly answered, 'if she was a twin.....How on earth would you be able to tell which witch, was which witch?'

Everyone enjoyed David's amusing remarks and Bill settled down to driving them further into Forest Valley and towards the Gemini Cave.

'Those poetic words I started to say earlier are so right,' Sylvia said, as they parked the car...... *'Neath a green leaf's mantle like sail, in the Forest and Valley's green dale.'*

'You're right, Mum,' Mary said, 'and that's so poetic. And I do like poetry.'

'We all like poetry, Sis, but there's no need to go over the top,' David said, as they started walking into the forest.

'Or complain over the top either,' Bill added. 'Both your mum and sister are really impressed by the forest, David. This truly is a beautiful place. Here we are on a hot sunny day in July, and beams of sunlight are streaking down through the various shades of dappled leafy green.'

David broke in at this point. 'You're joking, Dad, aren't you?'

'Just a little bit, Son. But you have to admit, it is a lovely afternoon and a really nice spot. You'd be hard pressed to find a more peaceful and naturally attractive place on such a pleasant July afternoon.'

'Steady on, Dad, this spot has really got you going.'

'Well, as I said earlier, your mum and I missed coming in here a few years ago because of a storm, so I am just soaking up the pleasant atmosphere now that I have the chance.'

They all put on their personal rucksacks which they always carried in the car and Bill led the way through the peaceful woodland along a path which led to a rock face rising up from the edge of the trees. Just before they reached the cave Mary asked her dad, and just before David managed to, how the cave got its name.

'The mythological story or folk legend that brought about its name concerns a young couple, their baby twins and Merlin,' Bill began. 'The background to the story, as I remember it, seems to be that Merlin wanted somewhere safe to hide the twin babies. Elders in the local village for some obscure reason had thought the twins were a bad and unlucky omen and that they were linked to black magic. Because of this they were seen as a threat to all the village farmers' crops and livestock and so had to be killed. Fortunately, the twins' parents somehow managed to contact Merlin. Merlin in turn removed the twins from the village having informed the elders, and much to their pleasure said he would save them the unpleasant job of destroying them.

'What in fact he did was hide them in the cave system we are going to visit. Their parents were then able to bring them up until they were old enough to leave. As a consequence, the cave in which the twins were hidden was named Gemini Cave by Merlin, after the Gemini constellation of the Twins.'

'I sometimes think you're a walking encyclopedia, Dad.' David said. 'But seriously, you do know so much interesting stuff.'

'That's why he's been so helpful to you two over the years,' their mum said, glowing with pride.

'It's got two entrances,' David remarked as they reached the cave, 'but then why should I be surprised that the Gemini Cave would have two entrances! The one to the right, and I don't know why, for some reason feels like the one we should explore.'

'We've all got torches in our rucksacks,' Sylvia said, as she took hers out, but we'll stay together and use my torch first. That way I can keep an eye on the lot of you,' she said smiling. 'Caves are the last place I want to be in if I lose track of any of you and you disappear.' She switched on her powerful torch and in they went.

'Be careful where you're putting your feet,' David said as he was the first to enter the cave. Somebody's...... '

'That's enough thank you, Son!' His dad interrupted him. 'We can all see what we need to avoid.'

They had only gone a little way in and just cleared the area lit by natural light, when Mary, who was now one step ahead of them, suddenly stopped and said in an excited voice, 'Look! Here on the wet, muddy floor. Large footprints! They look about size twelve. The odd thing is it's not a boot or shoe sole pattern though. It's ... it looks a like a human bare footprint.'

And sure enough, not only was there one, but three bare footprints were clearly visible in the thin layer of mud that covered much of the floor of the cave.

'Yes that is odd,' Sylvia said.

'It's more than odd, Mum,' David said. 'It's ... it's ... its wierdabnormanous!'

'Wierdabnormanous?' Mary loudly questioned.

'I think you might be right,' she then said with a laugh in her voice. 'Yes, David, you just might be right.'

'However you want to describe it,' Bill said, 'it's hardly the place for bare feet, is it? Who or perhaps even what might walk about in a muddy cave with nothing on their feet?'

'And there's more this way!' Mary said, walking slowly with her head down staring at the cave floor and now moving more to the right. 'There are four more here. But like the first lot, they stop at the wall of the cave.'

She then turned towards the others, a questioning and puzzled look on her face. 'They couldn't have walked through the wall of the cave...' She stopped for a couple of seconds. 'Or could they?'

Chapter Four

GLISTENING CALCITE CAVERN

Having heard her daughter's comment, Sylvia thought for a moment before answering. 'I don't think so, love. I can't think of anything or certainly not anyone who is capable of walking through the wall of a cave.'

'But I can,' David said in a very positive voice. 'I know I can, Mum!'

Bill joined in at this point. 'I think I know where you are coming from, Son. You think that in time you might be able to, but do you honestly think he, or it, really can walk through the stone wall of a cave?'

'Yes! I really do, Dad. I think Drossmire and all his mates, who or whatever they are, are capable of doing or achieving just about anything, including walking through stone. And that's what these footprints are certainly suggesting. I know its wierdabnormanous, but do you have another explanation?'

'It's hardly likely that someone, a normal visitor, would take their boots or trainers off to walk in here,' Sylvia said, so we can discount that as an option.'

'Let's explore a little further then,' David said. 'Who knows, we might find something else that's interesting.'

With that they all started to gingerly move forward further into the cave, David having also taken his torch from his bag.

'There are more footprints here,' Mary said, having once more stopped. 'In fact, there are quite a lot, some stepping away from the wall of the cave, and others seemingly going back through it!'

David suddenly grabbed Mary's hand, making her jump.

'What is it?' she said in a startled voice.

'I have an idea,' he said.

'You frightened me.'

'Sorry about that, Sis. But I want you to try something with me.' He looked her straight in the face and said, 'I want you to think you can... and put your hand into the wall of the cave. I'll do it at the same time.'

There was silence for a few seconds as Mary allowed what David had suggested to penetrate into her imagination. She then smiled and said, 'Okay, why not? It's something I have always wanted to do anyway, and like you, Bruv, I think we both now can.'

Together they astounded both their parents, and even themselves a little, by doing it. Their arms disappeared into the cave wall without a sound.

After looking at each other in pleased amazement, they next looked down at their feet and, as if they had done it all their lives, stepped into the cave wall and disappeared from their parents' sight. They re-appeared a couple of seconds later before Sylvia and Bill had even had a chance to speak. Then they remained motionless and silent for about five seconds before David spoke.

'I have to tell you, Mum and Dad, I tripped in the garage at home a couple of months ago and put my arm through the metal door, then pulled it back. It scared me a bit when I did it, so I haven't tried it since.'

Mary butted in. 'I did a similar thing about six months ago and my arm went through the bedroom wall. Like David, it frightened me too. So when David suggested we should try the cave wall together, I knew I probably could do it and guessed something had also happened to David for him to suggest it.'

Their mum still looked shocked. 'Have you any idea what it felt like to see my two children, as old as you are, just disappear as you both stepped into that cave wall?'

'You shocked and frightened both of us,' Bill remarked, not sure as to how he should feel.

'I'm sorry we scared you,' David said, 'but we had to try it and you saw that it worked. We can do it. We can now walk through solid objects. It's another incredible ability to add to our growing list. Now it's your turn. We would like you both to try it with us?'

'Ooh yes, Mum,' Mary said, 'you can come too, Dad, if you like,' she said smilingly.

Sylvia looked shocked at the suggestion as she turned to Bill. 'Do you think we could, love? Well...try it I mean?'

Bill, with a grin on his face said, 'Why not! I'm all for trying something different, and let's face it, this is different! It either will work or it won't. Yes, love, I'm all for it. We've got to give it a go. If we don't, we'll never know if we can or not. 'And he grinned broadly.

'Right then,' David said. 'Mary and I will hold hands as in twinning. You, Dad will grip my hand and Mum can grip Mary's...... We can then all step into the wall of the cave together!'

'You're sure about this?' Bill questioned. 'It isn't going to hurt either your mum or me?'

'Yes, we're sure we can do it, Dad,' Mary said, 'and no, it's not going to hurt. David and I are both confident we can do it. I feel sure we can make it work. My abilities say we can and I know I can trust them, so let's have a go.'

'We'll all stand close to the cave wall before we try,' David said, 'that way you won't bump your face if it doesn't work.'

So, gripping hands the way David had suggested, the Knight family placed themselves close to the cave wall.

'Okay?' David asked.

'Yes,' was the joint reply.

'Right, then let's do it. On three! One, two, three!'

Then they all attempted to step forward..... and succeeded!

It took two more paces being led by the twins for them to emerge into a large illuminated cave, about the size of two buses parked side by side. The lighting was being provided by six flickering torches, three on each side of the cavern.

It was an attractive cave with stalagmites on both sides the cavern floor, which looked as though they were reaching up, seemingly trying to reach the stalactites suspended from the ceiling of the cave, some of which were dripping with small rivulets of water.

Flow calcite had formed pale pink wavelike sheets down the rock face of the cavern walls and they glistened in the torch light. In some places the sheets had formed weird and wonderful shapes as they enveloped fallen rocks, making it all a real joy to see.

To say the expressions on all their faces were of shock and awe was an understatement!

David was first to speak. 'Well, that's a first. We did it! It seems we can do just about anything, Sis. Is everybody all right? Mum, Dad, are you both okay?'

'I don't think I'll ever be the same again,' replied

Sylvia, 'but yes, David. I'm okay, are you, love?' she asked addressing Bill.

'Yes, thank goodness, I am,' replied Bill, 'that really was something else. What's that word, David? Brillfanmagical!' They all laughed. 'But where are we?'

'And who lit the torches?' Sylvia asked.

'Probably the owners of those bare feet,' David replied, 'but who are they, and what are they doing here?'

'Cavemen died out thousands of years ago,' Mary said, 'but if they are part of Drossmire's group or forces, they could have been supernaturally re-created.'

'But this cave obviously isn't part of the known cave system,' Bill said, 'so we need to decide quickly whether we want to explore more of it or go back.'

'I think we have to accept that all of this has probably been created supernaturally, as you suggested, Dad,' David said, 'but I'm for exploring a bit further if we all agree.'

'We need to find out why they have done it if we can,' Mary added, 'so like David, I think we need to explore just a little more.'

'Okay then,' Bill said, 'but let's proceed with real caution. We've no idea what we might find or what or who we might meet.'

They all agreed, and with all the torches now switched on, they slowly moved forward towards the end of the glistening cavern to where it narrowed to a head high tunnel.

'I can never remember which ones are the stalagmites,' Mary said, as they moved gingerly across the floor of the cavern.

'Surely you can remember, it's tights that come down,' David said laughing.

'I think that's more than enough, David,' Bill broke in to say, 'and we know the rest of it thank you.'

Mary innocently said she didn't, so Sylvia suggested they left it there for now, saying she'd talk to her later.

They had almost reached the entrance to the tunnel when, taking them all by surprise, two tall, long-haired, clean shaven men with athletic physiques like Hercules, literally stepped out of the wall. Both were wearing black loin cloths and each brandished a small stalagmite in his right hand.

'They look like trouble,' Bill said.

'I couldn't agree with you more, Dad,' was David's comment, as he suggested they step back a couple of paces. 'We come in peace,' he began nervously. 'We mean no harm. Take me to your leader… Sorry everybody, I didn't mean to say that. I just couldn't think of anything else to say. I must have seen it on TV or in a film or something.'

But he needn't have worried, for the cavemen, or whatever they were, hadn't moved. They remained absolutely motionless.

It then became only too obvious as to why. The shadows of two other figures were now being cast on to the floor of the cave by the burning torches, as two more men of similar appearance but wearing white loincloths were slowly approaching behind them. They too had stalagmite weapons which they were now raising.

'Quickly, step to the side of the cave everybody,' David hissed as he pulled his mum to one side. Mary did the same with her dad on the other side of the cavern, as they suddelnly realized what was about to happen.

Seemingly the Gods of the Terrestrial Light, who watched over everything, had seen that their special Terrestrial Twins had been taken by surprise. Wanting to show that they were still keeping an eye on things, they had sent in a couple of warriors of their own to add to the

Knight family's defence and ensure their safety. The Knight family was obviously going to be needed for something more important.

The fight that ensued was rather violent and a bit bloody, but the two cavemen who had stepped out of the wall were no match for the two warriors the gods had sent, and it wasn't long before it was all over. After being slain, the two dead bodies dissipated in that all too familiar way of two years ago. All that was left was a gooey pool of slimy muddy mucus, and two equally slimy, muddy loincloths.

The two good-guys then smiled, bowed and faded, leaving the four family members on their own once more.

'I think we were cleverly ambushed,' David said. 'They somehow knew we were coming, didn't they? We were duped to come in here. They left those footprints in the mud in Gemini Cave knowing we would be tempted to try a cave wall walk.'

'Cave wall walk?' Mary mused. 'I like that. Cave wall walking, yes, I do like that.'

David smiling continued, 'Yes and we all fell for it. Without doubt, we are up against a really sly villain. He intends to challenge us as well as defeat us. Perhaps he sees all of it, whatever it is going to be, as one big game.'

'I'm pleased the Terrestrial Light Gods were keeping an eye on us,' Bill said. 'Would you and Mary have been able to defeat those cavemen, David, if we hadn't received help?'

'Yes, Dad, no problem,' David replied. 'I have no doubt in my mind as to our capabilities. Have you, Sis?'

'Yes, I agree with you, Bruv. I also am confident we are more than capable of looking after ourselves, especially as we keep realizing we have more or stronger abilities. Two years ago we flew, zapped goblins with lightning blasts from our fingers, reduced our size to inches, called up King Arthur's Sir Gawain and Robin Hood, and we also had a red dragon and a supernatural cow to help us. We even managed to get rid of a load of goblins that did their best to kill us all, and we even saw off King Offalmire. This year we have added cave wall walking. So, when you add all these supernatural abilities to our martial arts skills, it makes me feel we could take on just about anything.'

'Well, if you put it like that,' Sylvia said, 'we've all got to feel a lot happier and safer.'

'But can you get us out of here?' Bill joked. 'I think we've been in this cavern long enough. And another thing, it isn't very warm in here and I think your mum is feeling the cold a bit. I know I am.'

Having put their torches in their bags, they grasped hands and effortlessly walked through the cave wall and back to the place they had started from, a little way inside the entrance to Gemini Cave.

On the way back to the car, David, who had been deep in thought, surprised them all by saying, 'What if the voice that sounded like Merlin and talked to us wasn't? What if it was Drossmire impersonating Merlin? He virtually suggested we visited the caves. He enticed us in. He dangled the bait and we took it!'

'But it might have been Merlin,' Mary said. 'It sounded a lot like him.'

'We'll know sometime in the near future,' Bill said, 'we'll be in Castershire later this afternoon. We'll head back to the main road now then go straight on to the holiday cottage.' Then, addressing the twins, he asked. 'Do either of you want to drive?'

'Thanks, Dad, but David can drive. I've got a bit of an annoying headache.'

'Thanks, Sis,' David said. 'You can drive tomorrow.'

They all climbed into the car and headed for their holiday cottage Castershire, David behind the wheel.

As they were approaching the Forest Valley Road Tunnel, Bill reminded them of what had happened last time, just after they had entered it.

'Do you think it's remotely possible that it might happen again, Dad?'

'I don't know, Son. Why don't you try to recreate it or ask for it to happen? If you don't ask you will never know whether or not it might be repeated.'

'That's a brill' idea, Dad. I think I will.'

Having decided he would try to recreate what their parents experienced two years earlier as their car entered the tunnel, David said, 'Please, Gods of the Terrestrial Light, could you kindly recreate what happened in here two years ago when Dad drove through, so Mary and I can enjoy the experience as we were both sleeping and missed it?'

At first they thought nothing was going to happen, but just before they reached the end of the tunnel, and just as it had done two years earlier, their car was again suddenly engulfed in a blinding ball of white and pale blue shimmering light. The car then shuddered and lifted a couple of feet off the road and simply disappeared in a beautiful rainbow glow.

'Wow!!' David and Mary said together.

But it didn't end there. Brief images of supernatural events they had all experienced two years earlier flashed up and around them, rather like a fast-forward replay, giving them brief glimpses of previous incidents and scary involvements... David tangled underwater, Mary and her mum in a muddy hole, dodging a knife, fighting on the lawn, being circled by goblins and an adder attack. Mary stuck in sand, Offalmire blocking the road, the collapsing monolith, the waterspout and the dragon, a badger transforming into Merlin, a policeman goblin blasting them with a shotgun, the poison ingredients, naked dancing and a fight to the death at Moatcaster Castle.

And then, in a final flash of bright light, it all finished and their car materialized outside their holiday cottage. Again they had been supernaturally transported to Castershire. What next?

Chapter Five

OBSERVED ARRIVAL

They remained in their seats in complete silence for what seemed ages, but which was in fact only about twenty seconds, each thinking about the events of which they had all just been reminded.

David spoke first. 'Brillfanmagical! It really was!'

'I'll not argue with that,' his dad said.

'It would be difficult to,' added his mum.

Mary, still looking a bit shocked said, 'Well, you did ask them to recreate what happened two years ago. And wow! Didn't they just! And would you believe it, my headache's gone.'

'We really did do all that though, didn't we?' David said, as he switched the engine off. 'What a fantastic holiday and mythological and supernatural adventure that was! It was nothing less than brillfanmagical! And the way things are going so far, we could be in for another supernatural adventure to remember.'

Then they all turned to see Ector, the owner from whom they had rented the cottage for their holiday. He looked as though he was glued to the spot. He was standing close to the cottage door dressed as usual in soiled green overalls and leaning on a garden hoe he held in his left hand.

He somehow had witnessed their car materialize outside the cottage, and now, with his eyes wide open, he seemed transfixed to the spot. He looked rather like a statue which had been dressed in working clothes.

Bill and Sylvia got out and walked round the car, a smile on both their faces. Bill held his hand out to shake hands with Ector and to see how he would react to his approach.

'Hi, Ector! Good to see you again. We missed you last time we were here. You had broken your leg and were in hospital. I hope it's all right now. And how's Joyce?' Bill was now referring to Ector's wife. But Ector still didn't move, so Bill tried again.

'We spoke to her on the phone and thanked her for the Christmas card and the twins' birthday cards.' But it was no good. Ector just kept staring at their car, which was now almost empty as the twins had been busy taking out the luggage.

Sylvia then spoke to him. 'We're having our holiday a bit later this year. The twins wanted to take their motorcycle tests and driving tests before we came on holiday, but couldn't until they were seventeen. So we agreed to defer coming to your lovely cottage until now, near the end of July rather than in late June.'

She had obviously tried to get Ector to re-focus his mind off the car. But whatever they said, it wasn't working. He was motionless, transfixed.

'Let's face it, Dad!' David said, 'it's not every day you see a car, any kind of car, just appear out of thin air in front of you. There's no wonder he's... well, transfixed.'

'But what are we going to do about it, Son?' Bill asked. We can't leave him like that. And how is he going to cope with what he has seen when he eventually does come round? You and your sister have got to think of something.'

'But he shouldn't have been able to see it happen at all, should he, Dad? What we do supernaturally should be out of sight or earshot of normal humans.'

'Yes, that's true,' Sylvia said, 'but the fact remains, he did see us arrive out of thin air. Just look at him poor thing. He looks like he's frozen to the spot. Isn't there anything you can do or try?'

'I have an idea,' Mary said. 'You just said he looks like he's frozen to the spot. Well, let's unfreeze him. We could try twinning and tell him to forget what he's seen and to return to continue his life as normal. It could be as simple as that and it just might work! Our powers might allow us to do such things, but up to now we haven't had a reason to try.'

'That's a good idea, love.' Bill said. 'We've nothing to lose. And we just can't leave him like that.'

David, grasping hold of Mary's hand, stood close to and behind Ector and whispered into his ear. 'We ask the Gods of the Terrestrial Light to free this man of the memory of what he witnessed. Erase the event completely from his mind and allow him to carry on his life as normal. Thank you.' They then stepped back.

They were all both pleased and relieved to observe Ector blink a few times, then turn to speak to Bill.

'Hello! Welcome to Castershire again. I hadn't noticed you'd arrived. I must have been miles away with my thoughts. It must be an age thing! He reached out and shook Bill's hand.

'You're a bit later this year aren't you?'

'Better late than never,' Sylvia replied.

'I'll leave you to get unloaded. Oh, and Joyce sends her love. She keeps saying, "Break a leg," but I don't want to do that again!' And mumbling something to himself about a flash of light he walked away.

'Another first,' Mary said, 'thankfully that worked well, but I don't know what we would have done if what David tried hadn't worked.'

'Me neither!' David replied. 'But it really does look as though if we ask for the help of the Terrestrial Light Gods, and they agree with what we are requesting, we can do almost anything.'

'Does that frighten you?' Bill asked. 'Or you, Mary? Are you happy with that?'

'Yes, I think I am,' Mary replied. 'The extra wisdom we have been blessed with allows me to understand that neither I nor we would do anything we shouldn't.'

'That's the way I feel about it too,' David said. 'I feel confident that I wouldn't want to do anything that wasn't readily acceptable to you, Sis, or you, Mum and Dad, or anyone else for that matter.'

'Except Drossmire,' Mum said. 'I'm sure you could think of something he wouldn't find too acceptable.'

The guys finished unloading the car then sat down for tea and sandwiches prepared by Mum with Mary's help.

During tea, David again brought up the fact that Ector had witnessed their supernatural arrival, questioning his parents about it. Like the twins, however, their parents were still a bit stumped until Sylvia suggested that Ector, unknown to them, could possibly be a white witch, or was possibly descended from white witches. Both of these suggestions were acceptable reasons as to why he had been able to see their car when it materialized, literally out of thin air.

'Good thinking, Mum,' Mary said. 'Now it makes sense. But it must have really shocked him when it first happened.'

'Does that mean that all white witches might be able to see what we can see?' David mooted. 'If they can, it could be that someone else might witness something we might get involved in.'

'That's a good point, Son,' Bill said, 'but at the moment it's a hypothetical one. Perhaps it might be best to leave it like that until, or unless, something else similar happens.'

'I think your dad's right, David,' Sylvia said. 'Let's just get on with our holiday and with whatever it is Merlin might want us to do. I think this might be a good time kids for you two to try and reach him again.'

'Good idea, Mum,' David said. 'Come on, Sis, let's twin-up and see if we can contact him.'

Sitting down on the comfortable rose-patterned couch they had come to love, the twins grasped hands in a crossed hands twinning position.

'Hello, Merlin,' Mary said. 'We're here at our holiday cottage now. Do you have a message for us?'

There was a short pause before the pleasant and friendly voice of Merlin seemed to fill the whole of the room. But it was obvious by the expressions on all the Knight family's faces that something was not quite right and behind his soft words they detected a tension in his voice they were unfamiliar with.

He then asked them to look at the television. As they did, he appeared in colour on the screen. The picture showed him sitting in a poorly lit room with a stone wall behind him. His usually smart blue and white robe looked grubby and a bit worse for wear.

'Hello, Mary and David, and your lovely parents, Sylvia and Bill. I am so pleased to hear from you, especially as you are here in Castershire.'

'But you knew we were coming, didn't you?' David asked in a surprised voice. 'We spoke to you earlier in the week when we were still at home.'

The TV picture then turned black and white and Merlin changed to the form of a badger.

'And this morning too,' Mary said, having interrupted David, 'in the car after we'd had lunch.'

'No!' said Merlin, still looking like a badger and sounding somewhat surprised. 'I obviously knew you would be on your way here. But no, I haven't spoken to you recently at all, anywhere or at anytime. I was unable to, seemingly until you arrived in this area. I am not very pleased or proud of what has happened, so I ask you to be patient with me for a few moments while I explain.'

The Knight family looked around at each other blankly as Merlin changed back to his normal appearance and the TV picture changed back to colour.

'Someone who is proving to be a real threat to us all has tricked me. Someone whose identity I only learned for the first time yesterday. Up to then he had remained a secret.'

The TV picture again turned black and white, Merlin again appearing in the form of a badger.

'It appears King Offalmire had a son, whose name I only discovered yesterday from one of my captors.'

'But you told us on Wednesday about him,' David broke in to say. 'You said his name was Drossmire and he'd absorbed strengths and powers from his father's gooey remains.'

'No, David, I didn't!' It must have been the crafty Drossmire who contacted you, pretending to be me.'

'And he almost succeeded in having us ambushed in a cave,' broke in Mary.

Bill came in at that point, 'But what do you mean by captors? Are you a prisoner?'

'Sadly yes, Bill I am,' was Merlin's surprising reply. 'At the moment I am a prisoner in a dungeon below the north east tower in the Stonecaster Castle ruins, known as the black dungeon.'

'But how, and why?' Sylvia asked. 'Why you, Merlin, and how did they manage to do it?'

Merlin answered sorrowfully. 'I became rather distressed on Monday when I learned that the badgers whose sett I share were to be killed in a cull as part of an extended pilot badger cull being organized by the local council. So when those who were going to do it arrived, I transformed myself out of my badger disguise and into the form of a naturalist observer, intending to voice my objections and protect my friends.

'Sadly I was captured in a magical net that had been especially prepared for me by Drossmire. The supposed badger cull had been a clever ruse to entice me from the safety of the badgers' sett, and sadly it worked. I was then supernaturally transported by my captors to this dungeon below the ruins of Stonecaster Castle.'

'And was it Drossmire who planned it all, Merlin?' enquired Bill.

'Yes, I'm afraid it was, Bill. I was tricked and taken totally by surprise. He's probably listening even now he's so cunningly clever.'

The TV picture and Merlin's image continued to change as it flicked from a black and white picture to colour and back again.

'We'd better come and get you out!' David said. 'There is no way we can leave you in there.'

'But you will be in grave danger if you try,' Merlin said. 'It is obvious Drossmire is up to something and hopes you will try to free me and in doing so, perhaps die in the attempt. It all feels like an evil trap.'

'That's enough talk for now,' Bill said, 'we're only about ten to fifteen minutes from where you are. We'll come and get you out.' The TV then turned itself off.

'Is it really as near as that, Dad?' David asked.

'Yes, Son, it is. We're only a few miles from Stonecaster so it won't take us long.'

'Do we need anything?' Sylvia asked.

'No, Mum,' was Mary's reply, 'nothing.'

'Sis is right, Mum,' David said. 'We both think we are pretty capable of coping with anything now. Let's go and release Merlin from... what was it he called it?'

'The black dungeon,' Bill replied.

'It sounds a terrible place,' Mary said.

'And it looked a terrible place on the TV,' Sylvia said. 'But this time we won't be taken by surprise.'

Bill had been right. It only took them a short time to get to the Stonecaster Castle ruins. Having found a place to park, they took the path that led into the ruins of what had been a rectangular medieval stone castle with four towers, one at each corner.

Below what had been part of the main building were the almost intact remains of a large kitchen and pantry with a vaulted stone ceiling. All of which were visible through the doorway through which they peered.

'I don't see anybody,' David said, 'but I feel there is some sort of danger.'

'Me too,' Mary said. 'There really is a feeling of foreboding. We'll have to be careful, very careful.'

They had just turned away from the pantry, when out of the ruins of the south west hall and tower, about sixty yards away, emerged a ferocious pack of black and white, red-eyed snarling, barking and baying hounds. So the Knight family sensibly and quickly ducked in and under the pantry's arched roof to escape the growling onslaught of the evil four-legged animals as they bounded across the central section of the castle towards them.

David and Mary then joined forces to quickly create a safety barrier round them which effectively sealed off the doorway and the room's two window holes.

'It's a good job you two can create these safety bubbles round us,' Bill said, 'or we would all be gonners. Just look at the teeth in their snarling jaws. Those dogs have really been trained to kill.' The vicious hounds continued to jump, scratch and bite at the magical barrier with their sharp teeth in their slavering jaws, but fortunately their efforts were unable to have any effect.

'Yes, thank you, twins,' their mum said, 'you've saved us again. But how are we going to get out of here now, let alone get Merlin out?'

But the twins came up with a plan remarkably quickly. After having looked at each other and having smiled as they mentally communicated, they knelt down close to the doorway through which most of the hounds were attempting to gain access. Then they really surprised their parents. They started to loudly hum! Yes, they started to hum! And it was obviously the right thing to do. For what had seemed to be a most unusual thing to do, it somehow miraculously started to slowly do the trick. The hounds began to quieten down. The red glow also cleared from their eyes, and in a short space of time they became totally subdued and were unbelievably even wagging their tails!

'Good dogs!' David said. 'Good dogs! Thank you for quietening down. You all now realize who we are. We are the Terrestrial Twins and it was very wrong of you to try to kill us, any one of us. But we forgive you as we realize it wasn't your fault. You were demonically possessed by supernatural forces and made to do it, so you were unable to do anything about it. But you certainly can now! With our help, as you are all black and white, you can easily rid yourselves of your evil master. From the welts and scars visibly showing on most of your backs and ribs, it is only too obvious he has mistreated and badly beaten most of you. But now, if you choose to, all of you can change the situation.

'Through the power of the Terrestrial Light Gods we can give you the power to reverse what your master wanted you to do. You can now get rid of him instead, then disappear to a happier place with our blessing.'

The shabbily dressed individual who had been whipping the hounds, having overheard what David said, turned to make a hasty but unsuccessful retreat. He ran for his life back towards the ruins from which he and the hounds had emerged, the baying and growling dogs were hot on his heels, retribution the only thought in their minds. He had just managed to reach the ruins of what had been the south west tower when they caught up with him.

The noise of his ear-wrenching screams, amongst the snarling, snapping, growling and barking of the revengeful hounds, eventually ceased as Drossmire's helper was torn to pieces. The hounds then disappeared.

'I reckon he bit off more than he could chew,' was David's closing remark.

'Well done, you two!' Bill exclaimed.

'Yes, thank you,' their mum remarked. 'It was a surprise and a bit different what you did, but it did the trick all right, and that was good enough for me.'

'Some trick!' Mary exclaimed. 'But we still have to find and rescue Merlin.'

'I don't see anyone else out there,' Bill said. 'Perhaps they or he thought the hounds would have done the trick and got rid of us, so they didn't need a back up plan.'

'And oddly enough, I don't feel threatened anymore either. In fact I'm not sensing anything, are you, Sis?'

'No I'm not... Not a thing. But they might have a guard posted underground. Just because were not sensing anything up here doesn't mean there isn't anyone at the dungeon.'

Leaving the pantry cellar ruin, they walked round to examine the north east tower remains, speculating about the black dungeon being hidden below it.

'I don't think we have an alternative, David,' Mary said. 'We'll have to transport ourselves down to the dungeon and find out what is happening and be ready to deal with anything we meet down there.'

'I totally agree with you, Sis,' was David's reply. Then gripping Mary's hand he said, 'Let's do it!' And they both vanished...

Chapter Six

MERLIN DECEIVED & IMPRISONED

Having disappeared from the surface level of the castle ruins and their parents' company, the twins materialized underground in what looked like the old dungeon they had seen on their TV screen. But there was no sign of Merlin. It had been less than an hour since they had seen an image of him sitting uncomfortably in the dungeon while he talked with them. But the dungeon was now sadly empty. There wasn't even a guard for the twins to grapple with, and both of them were keyed-up ready for action.

Mary then spotted a note lying on the old scruffy, straw stuffed mattress and having picked it up, she read it. Passing the note to David she said, 'You read it. It might make a bit more sense to you than it does to me.' He took it from her and read it out loud.

'Do you remember the hoodie you killed earlier this week in your garden and what you said, David? Well, I have to inform you, Merlin has left the building.'

David, now rather annoyed, shoved the note deep into his pocket and after grabbing his sister's hand they transported back to the surface where their parents were nervously waiting.

Then in an angry voice David said, 'Merlin's not there. That rotten swine Drossmire is playing with us! He's setting traps and using Merlin as bait, hoping we will all be killed.'

'But are you two all right?' Sylvia asked in a rather nervous voice.

'Yes, Mum, we are, we're fine,' Mary replied, 'we're both fine. There was no one down there. No guards and more to the point, no sign of Merlin either.'

'That is if he ever was here, Sis!' David exclaimed. 'We may have just been tricked into believing he was here so that the hounds would kill us. On the other hand, he may have been here and now been transported somewhere else.'

'Well, if he's not here,' Bill said, 'where might he be?'

'Sadly neither of us has any idea at the moment, Dad. We haven't got a clue.'

'David's right, Dad,' Mary said, 'but as we have no idea at the moment where he might be, I suggest we go back to the cottage and see if we can contact him. Until we have, I think we need to put off our rescue mission until tomorrow. We'll all be feeling a bit more awake then than we do now, and that way we'll also have a full day ahead of us.'

'That makes an awful lot of sense, love,' Sylvia said. And as everyone also felt it was the sensible thing to do, they set off back to their cottage.

'I think we should try and contact Merlin again,' David said as they walked through the door. 'That way, we will at least be able to hopefully put his mind at rest, if we let him know what we are planning to do. That is if we are able to reach him.'

'It might put our minds at rest too,' Sylvia said, 'and that would help all of us to get a good night's sleep, especially as we're likely to be active tomorrow.'

Sylvia suddenly stopped what she was saying and was startled to hear a gentle tapping on the window. They all wheeled round to see four magpies sitting on the windowsill. So Bill carefully opened the window to talk to them.

'Hello magpies! It's been a little over two years since we last saw you. We hope you are all okay. Have you brought some news for us?'

'Good evening,' the magpie replied, as they had magically blended into being one bird while Bill was speaking to them. 'Welcome once more to Castershire, and yes, Bill, we do have some information for you. We have just learned that Merlin was never in Stonecaster Castle's black dungeon. He is in fact imprisoned in a dungeon situated in the base of the gatehouse at Leybent Castle, which is not far from Stonecaster village.'

'I knew it!' David blurted out. 'Drossmire is playing with us. He did set a trap using Merlin as bait for the hounds to kill us...'

'Or,' Mary butted in saying, 'is he testing our strengths and abilities? He really knows as little about us as we do of him, but he is certainly getting a picture now.'

'You could very well be right, love,' Bill said, 'and talking about pictures, I think you two should, as you suggested, try to contact Merlin again. Talking to him on the TV set was a bit special even though we were misled.'

'It will certainly help put our minds at rest and help us all get some sleep if we know what is really happening, and also what we might have to do to resolve the situation.' Sylvia, acting in her role as the family matriarch, found herself repeating what she had said earlier.

Bill thanked the magpie and suggested the twins get on with doing their thing, trying to get in touch with Merlin.

All of them were pleased and relieved when their telepathic efforts worked, and again Merlin's image appeared in colour on the TV screen.

'Thank you for calling and getting in touch with me, I thought it was today that you were arriving. Did you have a good journey?'

There was silence for a few seconds before Mary asked, 'But didn't we speak to you earlier today, Merlin?'

'No,' Merlin replied with a puzzled look on his face, 'I haven't spoken to you since...' He paused, clearly trying to recollect when they had last spoken. 'Since you were last here,' he said at last. 'Just over two years ago, the day you rid the world of King Offalmire in Moatcaster Castle!'

'Not at all today?' David asked, some tension understandably now showing in his voice.

'No, not once today nor since that special day two years ago in the castle. But from what you are saying, it is obvious someone has very cleverly been impersonating me. The only person I can think of who might be capable of such supernatural trickery is King Offalmire's son, Drossmire. I only recently learned of his existence and planned to talk to you about him when you arrived. He is fiendishly clever and deviously dangerous. I have to admit he actually caught me in a magical net and, as a result, sadly I am now imprisoned in a dungeon which is encapsulated in a strong supernatural barrier and I am unable to escape! For the time being even my own powers are unable to break the spell and I feel embarrassed for being such a gullible prisoner.'

David butted in at this point saying they knew the story, or thought they did, and had become only too well aware of the evil and cunning of Drossmire. They now realized he had been expert enough to have deceived all of the Knight family, not just once, but already on a number of occasions.

'But how do we know you are who you say you are, the real Merlin?' David then asked. 'You might be an imposter trying to deceive us.'

'Yes,' Mary followed David's thinking, 'How can we be sure now that you are the real Merlin? You could be Drossmire trying to deceive us again. It's all getting very complicated and a bit scary.'

'You twins have a good point there,' their mum said. 'We have to be sure!'

'Where are you now, Merlin?' Bill asked, attempting to focus his mind on the job in hand.

'I am sorry to say I am a prisoner in a dungeon below the gatehouse in Leybent Castle, Bill. Drossmire has already transported me on a number of occasions. I think in an attempt to confuse me. But I feel confident that my powers can accurately detect where I am. I have been in this location for two days. I have tried in vain to contact you a number of times to explain to you what was happening. Particularly when I sensed you were trying to reach me. But I was unable to penetrate the shield he had created around me. He really is a formidable opponent, and that is the way I think he sees himself.'

'I have an idea,' David said, 'I think I can prove whether you really are Merlin or not...What then, Merlin, if you really are Merlin, did you give to our mum as part of the poison potion, and what name did we give to your dragon?'

'Good idea, Bruv,' Mary commented, 'that should do the trick.'

Merlin's face lit up with a broad grin when he heard the questions. 'That's easy, David. Firstly, my gift to your mother: when I gave her the parchment tied with black ribbon which listed the poison ingredients, I also gave her one of them, a tuft of badger hair. As for your second question, my, and now also your, friendly dragon loves being called Red. In fact, he has asked me to call him Red ever since you named him a little over two years ago, up the chute below the rear of the King's Banqueting Hall in Moatcaster Castle.'

'Great,' said David, 'that's more than good enough for me. Good evening, Merlin! We're really sorry you are a prisoner and Drossmire managed to deceive you as well as all of us! But we'll soon be able to do something about it because we are back here in Castershire.'

'Thank you, David, it is really wonderful to see you all and know you are only a few miles away. That really is good news. I now feel a lot happier knowing you all are here. But it is getting late in the day, so please do not try anything tonight. Leave it until tomorrow. I will look forward to seeing you all again then. I am tired, but I will now be able to sleep knowing my favourite Knights are not far away. So I say goodnight to you all.'

His image faded from the screen and the TV switched itself off, leaving the family in a thoughtful mood.

'Right,' Sylvia said, ever the practical one, 'that's it until the morning. I'll fix us all a bit of supper and nightcap drinks. Then we will all go to bed and try to get a good night's sleep.'

'You two had better strengthen the barrier around the cottage to ensure we don't get any unwelcome guests in the night. That would be the last thing we would want. They say tomorrow never comes, but it better had if we're going to rescue Merlin!'

Bill agreed with his wife 'This Drossmire guy is a really devious entity,' he added. 'He's already demonstrated he's a pretty formidable character, having cleverly deceived all of us and having managed to both capture and keep control of Merlin. We will all need to be on our toes tomorrow or we might end up becoming prisoners ourselves rather than rescuers…'

Chapter Seven

LEYBENT CASTLE DUNGEON

The Knight family was surprised they had slept so well knowing they would yet again be facing the unknown in their attempt to free Merlin. They even wondered if somehow Merlin had managed to help them to get a good night's sleep, knowing they were going to need all their wits about them in their attempt to rescue him.

Sylvia decided to cook a full English breakfast for everyone. As they always enjoyed the bacon, sausage, eggs, baked beans, black pudding and fried bread with toast on a side plate which she always cooked to perfection, this time with Mary's help, no one argued. Having buttered toast and marmalade with a mug of coffee to follow the meal was as good a way as any to complete the breakfast and a perfect way to start any day. Especially as they had no idea of how much energy they might need or when they might next get chance to eat.

Bill cleared the table and everyone thanked Sylvia for such an excellent breakfast. The twins washed and dried the dishes which Bill put away. They really were a close, loving family team.

It was a lovely day and sunny enough for them to feel comfortable in shorts. The four of them looked quite resplendent having decided to again wear their Seven Magpies Studio strip as they climbed into their car and set off to hopefully rescue Merlin from Leybent Castle.

'Where is the castle?' Mary enquired of her dad.

'It's only a couple or so miles north west of Stonecaster, love, so it's not far away and it shouldn't take us long to get there. I have only ever seen the castle once, and that was when I was looking for a trout lake in that area. But I have sat-nav to help me now, so we won't have a problem today.'

'It's quite an impressive ruin,' David said when they arrived at the castle. 'I'm not really sure what I expected, but it's in a pretty good state. In comparison to some others we've visited, as I just said, it's quite an impressive ruin. A lot of the original buildings seem to be in place.'

'What's the word, Son?' his mum asked.

'No, it's not brillfanmagical like Moatcaster Castle, Mum. That's a really special place for all sorts of reasons. But nevertheless, this place is impressive.'

The twins then strengthened the barrier they had earlier placed on the car to ensure their safety and to enable them to speak without being overheard by anyone or anything that might be lurking in the area.

'How do you want us to go about it?' Bill asked of the twins as they were getting closer to the castle.

'We first need to have a close look at the gatehouse,' replied David.

'Then see if we can detect any threats in the area,' Mary added. 'There will no doubt be some guards underground outside the dungeon, but we can sort them out when we get down there. I feel I should be giving somebody a good bashing for the way they have treated Merlin and the way we are being played with, but I very much doubt we'll find Drossmire down there. I somehow feel he won't be around today. Let's hope he hasn't left us a problem on the surface this time though. Or might that be too obvious a thing to do?'

'You have been reading my mind, Sis,' David said, a broad grin on his face, 'that's just what I was thinking.'

'It sounds to me like you two have got the situation in hand,' Sylvia said. 'Good! Let's hope we don't have too much trouble.'

'Do either of you sense any threats or problems at the moment?' Bill asked as they walked towards the castle's information board to see if they could glean anything from it that might be of use to them.

'No, Dad, neither of us is sensing any bad vibes at this moment in time,' Mary replied, 'which is a bit odd if this is where Merlin really is.'

'You could have a point there, Sis,' David said, 'if this is really where he is.'

Having pinpointed the information regarding the gatehouse, they also read that the ghost of a black lion was featured in one of the many stories in the castle's history and its various legends and folklores.

Just after they started to walk towards the tower adjacent to the gatehouse, having just learned the dungeons were beneath it, the twins suddenly stopped and simultaneously very loudly cried out.

'Yipes!' David exclaimed. 'We have certainly got some supernatural company now, it's just arrived and it's not far away. We don't know what or who it is, but we are both sensing strong threats from something somewhere close to us, and at least one of them is BIG!......VERY BIG!'

'I can't see anything or anybody,' Bill said, his eyes darting everywhere searching for he didn't know what.

'Me neither,' Sylvia said in a strained voice.

'We can assure you we now have more than one entity not far from us,' David said, 'let's hope there are not going to be too many for us to handle. I think we had our fill of entities wanting to fight us two years ago at Moatcaster

Castle, so let's hope it's not going to be a repeat of that epic battle.'

As there was no one in sight they kept slowly walking towards the gatehouse tower, furtively looking around them so as not to be taken by surprise.

'Do you think Drossmire is playing with you again?' their mum asked. 'It all seems to be a big game to him. It's almost like cat and mouse, we being the mice.'

'Well, it looks like we are again being treated like mice,' David said, a noticeable tremble in his voice, 'and he's chosen a big cat, a very BIG cat to play with us.' As he spoke he looked straight across the castle courtyard where about thirty or forty feet in front of them a huge and magnificent black lion had magically materialized out of thin air. The lion was almost the size of their car!

It looked straight at them for a few seconds before bounding forward to stop about ten feet in front of them. Having stopped, it sat back on its haunches, opened its huge, slavering mouth full of the biggest pointed teeth imaginable, and roared twice. Its horrendous deafening roars, which felt as though they were attempting to shatter their ear drums, were the most terrifying, blood curdling sounds they had ever had the misfortune to experience. The awful noise reverberated around the castle's walls. It was even louder than the noise King Offalmire had made when they were first confronted by him two years earlier.

The effect was instantaneous and they all stood perfectly still. Sylvia was doing her best not to tremble while she gripped Bill's hand so tightly his fingers almost turned white.

'Anybody got any good ideas?' Bill whispered.

But then it was Mary's turn to act completely out of character, just as she had following her nude chanting dance two years ago.

'Yes, I have,' she said.

She then frightened and amazed the rest of the family by fearlessly walking straight up to the huge beast. Having licked its lips a couple of times and blinked, as though it couldn't believe its own eyes, the huge lion looked down as Mary approached and then tilted its head to the left to better hear what she said.

'I don't know how Drossmire managed to persuade you to come out here and make a nuisance of yourself,' she said, 'because I feel you're not known for being a nasty lion at all, are you?'

Then, to everyone's amazement, the lion replied, its hot breath spreading over Mary, who just shuddered as it brought back the horrible memories of being too close to Offalmire's foul smelling body in the fight to the death in Moatcaster's Castle.

'You are absolutely right, young lady. And might I say, a brave young lady, Mary Knight. Yes, I know who you are, and no, I'm not known for being an evil lion. I just went along with the idea of frightening you just a little. There is no way I would ever want to kill or eat the Terrestrial Twins, nor either of your parents, as I am a dear friend of Merlin. Drossmire said he would put a barrier around the castle and prevent me from haunting it if I didn't help him distract all of you for a while, that is if I couldn't bring myself round to eating all of you. So as I had no intention of killing any of you, I simply went along with attempting to distract you.'

'Well, you certainly caught our attention,' David said, having joined his sister and having heard what the lion had said, 'we're here to rescue Merlin.'

'Yes, I know, but you are a little too late to do that,' the lion replied, 'they moved him when I first arrived here to distract all of you, but I have no idea where he has gone.'

'He's done it again,' David said in an agitated manner. 'Drossmire has yet again managed to deceive us. He's duped us by tempting us to rescue Merlin and he's moved him again. He was hoping in the meantime that we would all be killed, this time by the black lion.'

'Can I stroke your mane?' Sylvia asked, having now joined the twins with Bill.

'Of course you can, Missus Knight. I would deem it an honour, you being the mother of the Terrestrial Twins. In fact, I would be very happy if you would all be kind enough to stroke me a little before I leave. No other ghost or mythical creature has ever had the honour to be so close to the Knight family. You will be doing me a really big favour. I will be able to brag about it for centuries.'

So all of the family did as he asked, in fact Mary and her mum both took it to the next level by kissing the lion on both cheeks, and David and his dad shook his right paw before he faded, a broad and very happy grin beaming all over his huge black face.

'What a wonderful, almost unbelievable story he will now have to tell,' Sylvia said.

'Now that was different,' Mary said, 'and I think we also have something special to remember as well. That incident would make a terrific story for us. But who could we tell?

'That's going to be one for our Memories Scrapbook, Sis,' David remarked, 'but we still haven't been able to rescue Merlin!'

'What now then?' Bill asked, but he immediately found out when four men, looking a little like centurions and all wearing light armour and brandishing swords, came running out of the ruins. They then formed a menacing, slowly moving circle round the twins and their parents, but didn't move in.

'What do you two want us to do now, Son?' Bill asked, not really knowing what to say.

'Not quite sure at the moment, Dad,' was David's almost humorous reply. 'I sense that something's not quite right and I'm getting a strange signal, a message. I've a shrewd idea of who it's coming from and what it might be and might mean.'

'Yes, David, I feel it too, you could be right,' Mary said. 'I think we should do something now, before we end up in real trouble.'

'I have an idea,' David said, 'let's all join hands.' Realizing this was hardly the time or place for asking questions, everyone grasped the hand of the family member standing either side of them and they formed a circle.

Both parents were then taken totally by surprise when they vanished from where they had been standing and materialized in the dungeon under the Chapel Tower. They were even more surprised to find themselves standing next to where Merlin was seated on a straw mattress which was lying on a rough, wooden bed. Despite his less than salubrious surroundings, Merlin was happily smiling!

'I knew you would work it out,' Merlin said whilst being hugged by Mary.

'It is you, Merlin,' Sylvia said. 'You really are here.'

'Yes, it is me, Sylvia. I am here and I am so pleased to see all of you.'

'Moments after the lion told you I had been whisked away again, Drossmire brought me back. He was confident you would become the lion's lunch or, if not, would leave and go off for some lunch yourselves. So having brought me back here, he left to find something for himself.

'It was while we were transporting back again that I seized on the opportunity to mentally send a brief scrambled message to the pair of you, which I was confident you would figure out. And you did, because here you all are. I am sorry, Sylvia and Mary, that it is not more welcoming in here, but as you all know, I was not the one to choose this place.'

At that moment two of the entity guards who had been above ground, having realized what might have happened, appeared outside the dungeon door and, while making a lot of noise, threw it open. David and his dad were then quickly involved in an active fight, trying very hard to not get slashed by either of the swishing sword blades the two entities were flashing about. Mary and her mum were sitting this one out on the bed with Merlin.

Pinning their attackers' arms up against the door and door frame, David and his dad were able to successfully disarm their opponents, then by rolling over quickly each of them picked up a sword. Defeated, the guards simply faded away but were instantly replaced by the other two who still had swords. A sword fight was inevitable, and it took place in the area outside the dungeon.

The fight had only just begun when the whole of the cell was flooded with a green light accompanied by an horrendous gut-wrenching stench. And there, with his back to the rear wall of the dungeon and close to Sylvia, Mary and Merlin, stood a very big and really obnoxiously ugly being.

His appearance was that of half man and half wrinkled, grey wild pig. Like his obnoxious father, he had candles of snot running out of and dripping from his snout-like nose.

Drossmire had made his first smelly appearance, but it was only to be a brief one. Having seen what was happening, he quickly grabbed hold of Merlin with one hand and sadly Sylvia with the other. Sylvia thumped and kicked as hard as she could, doing her best to break free.

But Drossmire's grip was too tight. Taking his struggling captives with him, he then disappeared as quickly as he had arrived, leaving behind a revolting, almost toxic, smelly fart.

Unfortunately, Bill, having been distracted from the fight after witnessing his wife and Merlin being whisked away, had given his opponent a momentary advantage and he drew blood on Bill's left arm with a sneaky sword movement.

Although the twins knew they were only to use their special powers over and above their own skills and strength in real emergencies, they thought that what was happening now warranted special action. Having seen their mum and Merlin disappear before their eyes and seeing blood on their father's arm, the twins both saw red and zapped one of the two remaining swordsmen. Seeing the other zapped thug dissolve into a pool of muddy mucus and crumpled uniform, the last remaining swordsman simply disappeared.

Bill and David then joined Mary in the cell and sat either side of her. The three of them were now showing real signs of stress and shock. They had all witnessed Sylvia being dragged away from them by an evil, obnoxious and very clever being, to be taken to goodness knows where, and all of them were obviously very upset.

'WHAT THE HELL CAN WE DO NOW, TWINS?' Bill shouted in anger and total frustration.

'At the moment we honestly don't know, Dad,' David answered quietly trying to calm him down. Mary gave him a big hug after tying his handkerchief round his cut arm in an attempt to stop the bleeding.

But it was all a bit too much for her and she burst into tears. Her dad put his arms round her to give her a loving hug. David then joined in and hugged tightly onto both of them. While still hugging them he transported all of them to the car and seated his dad next to his sister so he could comfort her. Having got behind the wheel, David reached to grasp Mary's hand saying he was going to attempt to transport the car with everyone in it back to the cottage. Then they did just that! It worked! Another first!

'You sit with Sis, Dad,' David said when they got back to the cottage. 'I'll make us all a nice mug of coffee. We can then discuss what we should or might do next, whatever it might be. But we've got to do something, and soon! We've no idea where they are or what that......' Bill stopped him before he could say anything else.

'As you yourself suggested, David, let's just sit quietly for a minute or two to unscramble our thoughts and emotions, we can then perhaps develop a plan.'

Bill placed his arm lovingly round his daughter's shoulders; Mary occasionally giving out little sobs. He had never seen her so upset, but then she had never witnessed her mum being snatched literally from under her nose by a monstrous, obnoxious being like Drossmire either.

No one spoke until David took the mugs to be washed. 'What, if anything do you think we can do, David?' Bill asked in a rather sad voice. 'We've got to figure a way out of this, Son, and soon. We can't leave your mother and Merlin with that….. that hideous monster.'

'She will be very distressed by now knowing we will all be upset worrying about her. We know she's strong but she's only human, unlike that beast who took her, and I want her back.'

'We all want her back, Dad, but you're right. Mum is strong and very capable of looking after herself, so try not to worry too much. You know she wouldn't want that. It's a shame Drossmire's powers are swamping Merlin's as well as our powers at the moment, or he or we would be able to get them out.' As he spoke David suddenly began to smile. 'But I just might have an idea!'

Chapter Eight

THE GREAT ESCAPE

Having put it to them, David's idea both surprised and pleased his dad and Mary. Having given him chance to explain, they realized that although it was a little different, it might just work. And as there didn't seem to be an alternative, it really was worth trying.

The idea was that, although Merlin and Sylvia were being prevented from escaping from wherever they were imprisoned by supernatural forces, it might nevertheless be possible for a rescue party to get in.

The prospect of an imminent rescue seemed to cheer up Mary and she listened attentively as David proposed enlisting the services of the magpies once more.

'They could fly into the dungeon in Leybent Castle from where Mum and Merlin were snatched,' he suggested. 'Then by using their collective powers, trace the parallel time route Drossmire used to transport them away. That way the magpies will learn where they are now and we can then develop a plan to hopefully rescue them.'

Bill thought it was a brilliant idea, as did the magpies when the twins, accompanied by their dad, went into the garden and suggested it to them.

'It really could work, Bruv,' Mary said. 'How on earth did you think that one up, it really is a clever plan?'

'It must be that I was born a genius,' David joked, happy to see a smile on both his sister's and his dad's faces again.

The seven magpies then blended into one and shot off to do their bit.

'It's great isn't it,' Bill said as they re-entered the cottage. 'We can always rely on the magpies for assistance no matter what we ask of them. Nothing seems to beat them. We really are lucky to be involved with them and they ask for nothing in return. I wish there were more humans around who behaved like they do, the world would be a much better place.'

'Wow, Dad, such a philosophical comment!' David said. 'It must be because of Mum's situation eh? We don't often hear you talk like that.'

'I'm not sure, Son, but I expect so. But you have to admit, even though we know the magpies are our supernatural guardians, they are the perfect examples of what true friendship is all about and what it really means.'

'I know we won't feel like having much lunch, but we all need to have something to keep our strength up,' Mary said, having taken over Sylvia's role in her absence. 'Let's all get showered and changed into fresh magpies strip, and I'll bandage your arm properly, Dad. We can then decide what to eat.'

After opting for cheese sandwiches, pieces of cake and mugs of coffee, they all sat round the coffee table to have their snack lunch.

They had just finished and were about to clear the table when the magpie returned, flying in through the open door giving everyone a bit of a scare as it landed and settled on the back of the settee.

'That Drossmire really is an evil being,' it started. 'Would you believe he's also got two teenagers locked up as well as your mum and Merlin. I don't know where he snatched them from, but they are about your age and wearing shorts and tee shirts similar to the ones you sometimes wear.'

'But where are they? Bill asked.

'The young man is like you, David. He's got black hair.'

'But where?' Bill again asked.

'The young woman with him is rather attractive. Like you, Mary. She's also got virtually white hair and blue eyes.'

There was a pause as the magpie realized his audience was looking at each other with mixed expressions of surprise, shock and disbelief on their faces.

It was David who asked this time. 'But where, magpie? Where are they?'

'Sorry, David, I should have told you first, but I sometimes go on a little too much before I get to the point, especially if I'm excited.'

'Please! Where are they?' Mary said, joining in the questioning.

'Sorry, Mary, but as I said, I do go on sometimes.'

David looked as if he was about to explode with frustration when the magpie finally came out with what they all wanted to hear.

'They have all been transported to a dungeon below Tollvale Castle.'

'Thank you, magpie. Thank you very much for that,' Bill said with relief in his voice. 'Tollvale Castle eh? Fortunately, just like the other castles have been, it isn't that far away. We could, unless we meet any problems en route, get there in about fifteen minutes or so.'

'Just a minute, Dad,' David said, and addressing the magpie went on to ask, 'were you able to communicate with Merlin?'

'Yes. I remained invisible to make sure no one saw me, and I was able to link with Merlin's mind. He is tired and a little hungry, but he asked me to let all of you know that Sylvia was all right.'

'Did he say anything else at all?' Mary asked. 'What about the two strangers Drossmire has also snatched, surely he said something about them?'

'Merlin says they are here to possibly help you. I don't know how or why, but that is what he said, and he looks forward to seeing you all soon.'

'How many guards are there?' Bill asked.

'I saw three,' replied the magpie, 'and there was someone out of eyeshot, but I heard him or it moving about, but I have no idea who or what it was.'

'I wonder why he kidnapped those two teenagers' David questioned. 'And why are they here to help us, and how can they? At the moment it doesn't make a great deal of sense at all to me. Again it appears we have more questions than answers.'

'We'll find out later,' Mary said. 'But it can hardly be a coincidence that they are physically similar to us with the same black and white hair.'

'It's like you just said, Mary, we'll find out more about both of them later,' Bill said. 'What we really need to do now is to get over to Tollvale Castle as quickly as we possibly can. Are you ready?'

They all decided that going to the bathroom before they went anywhere would be a good idea. They thanked the magpie again for his help and he then disappeared.

'As I know the way, it will be quicker if I drive,' Bill said as they locked up the cottage. They had decided that transporting to Tollvale might not be a good idea, as their magical presence might more easily be detected. And off they went on yet another enforced rescue mission.

'That's a really smart looking house,' David said, as they descended the hill to the narrow, single-file traffic bridge which took them over the river and past Tinker's Hall.'

'The site has got a varied history going back around two thousand years,' his dad said. 'There are some interesting folklore stories and legends about the house though. There is supposed to be a friendly white lady ghost who haunts the building and the boathouse. But there's also another ghost, or *a something* that's not so friendly. A legendary tale tells of a tinker who's surname was Tinker and who lived in the house. It was from him the building got its name. Apart from originally being a tinker, he had at one time also been the owner of two trading ships and he brought back three alligators with him from his last trip to put in the hall's lake.

'The story goes on to say that he kept one of the poor creatures chained up and tormented and horribly ill treated it. He even at times starved it and subjected it to unspeakable cruelty and painful torture. Some stories say he regularly burnt it with torches because he liked the sounds it made when it roared in pain. It's the tormented alligator's ghost that is also supposed to haunt the hall's lake, particularly close to the boathouse.

'It has also been reportedly seen around the walled area, which was built to look similar to the inner walls of a castle. The person it was originally built for couldn't afford a whole castle and so made do with bits of one. Also, because that owner liked castles, he used to stage medieval style jousting tournaments there which were very popular.'

'You don't half know some interesting stuff, Dad,' Mary said. 'But let's get back to thinking about Tollvale Castle and its problems, as I'm sure we'll soon be there. But wasn't it when we were on the beach near that castle two years ago that Mum was attacked?'

'Yes, love,' Bill said, 'it was. So it might mean we are going to be facing some goblins or some sort of entities again, similar to the ones we met last time.'

'They were good fighters as well, if I remember correctly!' David said.

'Yes, Son, they were good, in fact they were very good. But we beat them then, and as we all know, you and your sister are now two years older and stronger and even more skilled at fighting than you were then. And let's not forget your much improved supernatural abilities either. I feel extremely confident that we will be able to cope with whatever physical problems we might encounter.'

As they arrived in Tollvale village Bill spotted a car moving out from a convenient spot and quickly pulled the car into the vacant spot.

'We didn't see the castle from this angle last time, did we?' Mary remarked. 'What's the word, David?'

'Brillfanmagical,' David replied, 'it's nowhere near as big as Moatcaster Castle, but it really is a splendid, imposing building.'

'There used to be a drawbridge here,' Bill said, as they approached and entered into the inner ward of the castle. But that's enough talk for now, let's concentrate on the job of rescuing your mum and Merlin. Oh yes, and those two teenagers! They're a bit of a mystery though, I must confess. Why were they kidnapped? I know we keep saying it, but it still doesn't seem to make any sort of sense. Well, not at the moment. But I am sure Merlin will have an answer.'

'I agree, Dad,' David said, 'we'll all soon know if we manage to get everyone out.'

'We've got to,' Bill said. 'Let's just hope that Drossmire hasn't moved them again.'

'I'm sensing evil,' Mary said.

'Me too, Sis, but I'm not sure how many there are.'

'Can't we try something different this time, David? I thought your idea was great, but I'd first like to try and transport them out from up here. Preferably without us having to go down to the dungeon first!' Mary shuddered involuntarily at the thought of another trip to a dank and dangerous dungeon. 'Going down to where they are seems to have given us problems when we've tried it before, so I thought we might try something different. And as you have already said, the barrier around them is to stop them from breaking *out*. It's not to prevent us from breaking *in*. If we ask the Terrestrial Light Gods to help, do you think we might be able to create a hole in the barrier from this side? We can then beam in and escort them out. With our combined efforts I'm sure we'll be able to free them. We've got to try it 'cos I feel sure it will work.'

'It's a good idea, Sis. No, it isn't, it's a great idea and really I like it... So why not? Let's give it a go. Today seems to be the day for good ideas.'

They both then clasped their hands tightly together in a twinning hold and asked that their mum, Merlin and the two teenagers be released from the dungeon and Drossmire's supernatural net and be allowed to appear on the grass alongside them.

Within three seconds, and encapsulated in a pale blue bubble that faded away as their feet touched the ground, all four people they had hoped to rescue stood beside them. With the help of the Terrestrial Light Gods they had done it. Drossmire's prisoners were free. It really was a great escape!

Sylvia ran to throw her arms round Bill who was already making a beeline for her. Turning to the twins, Sylvia beckoned them to join her so she could hug them too.

'What a clever family you are. Thank you. Thank you for rescuing us.' And she gave both twins a big kiss on the cheek.

'Yes, thank you so much,' Merlin said. 'I was beginning to think I was never going to be free and I was getting tired of constantly being moved from place to place. What you won't realize is that it took not only both your twinning power and mine to free us, but also a small amount of energy from these two. Two young people I would like you all to meet.'

And turning towards the teenage couple who had also been rescued he said, 'Allow me to introduce you to Gwen and Arthur. What none of you know is that they are also twins. They should have been born on the same date on the calendar a year before you two came into the world. But their mum had them prematurely, so their fifteenth birthdays no longer coincided with the Summer Solstice, and therefore they could not become the Terrestrial Twins, as had been planned for them to do. That honour then befell you, Mary and David, one year later. You could say they missed out.'

'Is that why, like David and Mary and me and Bill, their hair is black and white?' Sylvia asked.

'Yes.' answered Merlin. 'They, and not you two, were originally to become the Terrestrial Twins. The Gods of the Terrestrial Light thought King Offalmire would be able to get at the Thirteen Treasures of Britain a year earlier than when he eventually tried. But because of an illness he didn't become powerful enough until a year later than expected. So it worked out all right and you, Mary and David, received the honours that Arthur and Gwen missed, and were able to finally rid the world of Offalmire.'

'So do they have powers too, like David and Mary have?' Bill asked.

'No. Well, only like David and Mary had before their fifteenth birthdays, which were quite considerable really.

They just didn't know it. Both Gwen and Arthur were made aware of theirs two years ago, and I also had them strengthened and improved a little, just in case you twins needed some additional back up. But with your abilities and Sylvia's and Bill's assistance, plus a few others' help, you coped admirably. But they were here in Castershire all the time, just in case they were needed.'

'So you are eighteen-year-old twins?' David said, addressing Arthur and Gwen.

'Yes,' replied Arthur. 'And we both also thank you for getting us out of that dungeon.' And reaching out shook hands with both twins. 'And it's our pleasure to at last make your acquaintance.'

'You really did us a favour saving us,' Gwen said. 'Thank you. And it really is a pleasure to meet you both.' She then kissed David on the cheek having first shaken hands with Mary.

Bill was just about to speak when his would-be question was answered, as four entities emerged from the castle building dressed as Roundheads, each with a sword flashing in his hands.

'THEY'RE OURS, MUM AND DAD!' David shouted. 'LEAVE THEM TO US!'

To observe the two sets of twins with nothing other than their arms, hands, legs and feet as weapons take on four of Drossmire's armed warriors was a sight to behold. It was obvious from the way that both Arthur and Gwen reacted and fought that they too had also received martial arts training. The whole fight was almost like watching a perfect demonstration of how to deal with armed assailants!

What was quite a furious fight only lasted about three minutes as all four teenagers were pretty outraged at what had been happening to them, and particularly to the twins' mum and Merlin. They fought with such intensity and forceful skill that the sword-wielding attackers didn't really stand a chance and quickly came off worst. Each in turn lost his weapons which were picked up and expertly used by the twins.

The expressions on Arthur and Gwen's faces when they saw the bodies of their attackers turn into bubbling pools of snotty slime told the Knight family that they had never seen anything like it before.

'Do they always end up like that?' Gwen asked, turning to David.

'It's not a pretty sight, is it? But yes, they do, usually! We thought it really strange too, at first.'

'We've got used to it now,' Mary added. 'But it is a bit different, isn't it?'

'And did you see those outfits. I wouldn't be seen dead in something like that,' David joked.

Bill interrupted any other conversation by asking his twins to transport all of them back to the cottage rather than to drive back, just in case there were to be any surprises on the journey. So when the seven of them were seated in the car, all four twins linked hands and their car disappeared from its parking spot in Tollvale to re-appear at their holiday cottage...

Chapter Nine

A PERFECT END TO A DAY

Having arrived safely back at the holiday cottage, and once Sylvia had made sure everyone was comfortably seated, she prepared a pot of coffee.

'I do like your black four-wheeled carriage, it is rather splendid,' Merlin said, referring to their car. 'It is a most comfortable and useful means of transport. There was room for all of us to ride back here to the cottage.'

'Yes, it is comfortable, Merlin,' Bill replied. But he was too interested to know the full story about what had been happening to Merlin and who the new twins were, to continue to talk about their car. Having the new brother and sister twins mysteriously arrive on the scene had been a total surprise to everyone, so he knew the rest of the family would also be keen to find out where they fitted into the story.

'So,' Bill continued, 'allow me to sum up things to get my mind straight, Merlin. Until recently you had no idea Drossmire existed?'

'That is correct,' Merlin replied.

'And Arthur and Gwen were originally intended to be the Terrestrial Twins but were born prematurely so couldn't be?' Merlin nodded. 'And they have some powers, but nothing as strong as David and Mary's?'

'Correct. They are only small but useful ones which add slightly to their strengths and general abilities. They are nowhere near as comprehensive or as powerful as David and Mary's abilities since becoming the Terrestrial Twins, as their powers are superhuman powers. As Mary and David are directly linked to the Gods of the Terrestrial Light, their abilities are wide reaching. I think a modern word, "awesome", might get close to describing Mary and David's abilities. I just hope they never need to fully use all of them – once they discover and realize what they are! And the range and intensity of their skills will only continue to increase as they grow older.'

'Wow! Brillfanmagical!' David said, to the amusement of Gwen and Arthur.

'That's a new one on us,' Arthur said, smiling.

'I take it that's a special word of your own, David?' Gwen remarked, also grinning.

'Yes,' David replied, 'it's one of a number I invented just for fun a couple of years ago.' Then he went on to ask, 'So you two are eighteen?'

The other twins together replied, 'Yes.'

'Do you live in Castershire or are you on holiday?'

'We're here on holiday like you are,' Arthur replied, 'we're staying with an aunt in Stonecaster.'

'So you're not far away from our holiday cottage, where we are now,' Mary said with a big smile on her face that slightly puzzled David. Bill and Sylvia were not so naïve It was obvious to them that, even though she had only known Arthur for literally a few minutes, Mary was rather drawn towards him.

'Are your parents with you?' asked Sylvia.

'No, they were coming,' replied Gwen, 'but Dad broke both legs in a mysterious scramble bike accident, so they couldn't come. They knew Merlin had contacted us, so we came on our own. We hadn't been here long when Merlin's vibes reached us, asking us to go to Leybent Castle.'

'Yes,' Merlin said, 'as I knew the Knight family were coming here, and having suspected but not being sure that something might happen, I decided to ask Arthur and Gwen to come to Castershire as back up for you.' And with a twinkle in his eye he said, 'I also thought it a good idea and about time for both sets of twins to meet each other.'

'What did you say this drink was?' Merlin continued, addressing Sylvia. 'It is rather pleasant. I must get some.'

'It's coffee Merlin. I've got two jars. I'll give you one to take with you when you go.'

'Thank you, Sylvia. That is very kind of you.'

'So, what about Drossmire?' David asked. 'Is he about to break into the Crystal Tower to misuse the Thirteen Treasures, or is there something else we don't know about?'

'Having been forced to listen to him over the last few days,' replied Merlin, 'it appears the main reason for wanting you and Mary here, I'm sorry to say... is simply to kill you! Retribution is what is in his mind. You were responsible for his father's death. Now all he wants is to see you as corpses.'

'Well, you spelt that out clearly enough,' Bill said, 'he simply wants the twins dead. Is he not interested in the special Thirteen Treasures at all then?'

'As far as I can make out, although we must remember he is a very clever and devious entity,' Merlin warned. 'Retribution is without doubt his main reason for wanting you here, but as he is so devious and a most formidable enemy, I feel sure he also wants access to the Treasures. We really do need to devise a plan to rid the world of him, as you did with his father.'

'Well, there appears to be no urgency as to what might happen,' Bill said, 'so why don't we first enjoy a few days of our holiday? That will give us more time to discuss what our plans might be.'

'I think that's a sensible idea,' Merlin said, 'and I can now return to my badger sett. I thank you all once more for rescuing me. I will now be even more alert. I suggest you do the same. Call me if you need me. Thank you once more.' And he faded and was gone.

'He forgot his coffee,' Sylvia said. 'Whoever thought we would one day be sat chatting to the great Merlin and simply enjoying a cup of coffee in his company.'

'Right, you two,' Bill said addressing the Gwen and Arthur, 'I take it you arrived at Leybent Castle by car, and it's still there waiting for you?'

The twins replied, 'Yes.' So Bill suggested David and Mary should drive them back to pick up their vehicle.

'I have a better idea!' David said, 'we'll hold hands and magi-port into their car.'

'Okay,' said Sylvia, 'but please, all of you be very careful. I doubt Drossmire will be happy about losing all four of his prisoners, so please keep your wits about you. Our holiday has only just started. Let's hope we can all enjoy a lot more of it.'

Both sets of twins then stood in a circle facing each other and, having taken hold of each others hands, vanished.

An elderly couple passing near Arthur and Gwen's car had their attention suddenly drawn to it, for as the two sets of twins materialized in the car it bounced up and down a few times.

'Teenagers!' they muttered

The two sets of twins looked at each other and, having realized what the elderly couple were thinking, began to laugh, and for a little bit of naughtiness, bobbed up and down a couple more times to make the car rock even more.

'Mum would kill us if she knew we had done that,' Mary said.

'We'd better not tell her then,' David continued. 'It was only for an innocent laugh, but yes, we shouldn't have offended that couple. Our mum would certainly have been after us. Having Drossmire after us is more than enough! Sorry, Mum!'

They all enjoyed a laugh which did them the world of good. It helped take away the pressures of what had happened to them earlier and relieved some of the tension they were obviously still feeling, as they had no way of knowing what might happen next, or even when or where.

The ride back to where Arthur and Gwen were staying was fortunately also uneventful, and Arthur and Gwen ended up being just as astounded by that supernatural trip as they had been by the previous two.

'It looks like we missed out on a lot of things,' Arthur said addressing his sister. 'Wouldn't it be great if we could transport ourselves like that?'

But David butted in before Gwen could answer. 'It's not all fun and flying, Arthur, I can assure you.'

'No, David, I didn't expect for one minute that it was. But it is already very obvious we have missed out on so much by not becoming the Terrestrial Twins.'

'That's convenient,' Mary said in an attempt to bring the conversation back to normal. 'Our cottage is only about ten minutes from here, from your cottage I mean, which means none of us will have to drive very far to pick each other up. That is if you want to spend some time with us.'

'I think we'd both, love to!' Gwen quickly replied.

'Too true,' Arthur said. 'Meeting you has been an honour, and something else, but I'm not sure what. But I now feel we will all become good friends.'

'Good,' Mary said, 'what are you doing this evening then? We fancied doing a bit of carp fishing. There's a great pond near us. Do you fish?'

'We do actually,' Arthur replied, 'in fact we really enjoy it. What's the biggest you've caught?'

'We both caught an eighteen and a half pound mirror carp two years ago last time we were here,' David said.

'So did we!' Gwen said, and laughingly went on to say, 'Perhaps we all caught the same fish. So now we've all got to try and catch bigger ones.'

'As I now know where your cottage is,' Arthur said, 'it won't take us long to get to you either. We can make the fishing trip a bit of a competition if you like. The losers pay for lunch tomorrow in Moatcaster.'

'What a cool idea,' Mary said, 'let's hope it keeps fine.'

They all said cheerio. Then David and Mary transported themselves back to their holiday cottage. Or that is what they intended to happen, for as they disappeared from Arthur and Gwen's sight, something unimaginable, and they had no idea what, happened to them. All they could remember of the phenomenon was a pins and needles sensation over their entire bodies a split second before they blacked out.

When they came round, they had no idea of how long they had been unconscious as both of their watches had stopped. All they knew was that wherever they were, the pale blue light all around them was almost blindingly bright. David and Mary could sense they were not far from each other, but the powerful light made it impossible to see.

Fortunately, the atmosphere in which they now found themselves was pleasantly warm, as they realized they were totally naked and somehow horizontally suspended in thin air. Both their minds flew back to the time two years earlier when they were abducted in Lilymire Grotto, and they both now experienced an eerie sense of déjà vu.

As David felt he could telepathically communicate with his sister, he did. 'It looks like it's happened again, Sis. Are you all right?'

Maintaining her sense of humour, Mary replied, 'If waking up to find you have been undressed and are at the moment somehow suspended in thin air then yes, Bruv, I'm fine. Are you?'

Mary's comments made her brother, though obviously concerned, feel a lot better and he replied, 'Yes thanks, Sis, I'm Okay too, but it's not the same as last time though is it? I don't know if I have been examined or not. I can't remember anything, can you?'

'To answer your second question first,' Mary replied, 'I can't remember much after we experienced that pins and needles feeling, and no, it's not the same as last time. As for have I been examined, the answer is yes. I don't want to spell it out, but yes I know I have been examined but I have not been hurt in any way.'

'Good, I'm glad you're all right, Sis, fortunately so am I, but where do you think we are, any ideas?'

'Not really, Bruv, but I do sense we have been in the company of non-human entities. I have a feeling that this time they were more interested in our brains than our bodies – even yours,' she added mischievously. 'I'm presuming that you have been examined.'

'Can't remember, Sis, but as we both have yet again been abducted, it doesn't go far beyond the realms of possibility that the phenomenon of extraterrestrials exploring humans really is with us. That is, with the human race I mean.

'One thing that does bother me a bit though is, whoever they are, they can somehow negate our powers and I don't like that. But they obviously don't wish to hurt us or they would have done it by now.'

David had hardly finished communicating his last thoughts to Mary when their abduction was over and they materialized, thankfully fully dressed again, outside their holiday cottage.

'Not a word to Mum, David,' Mary said as they opened the front door. We'll talk about it another time.'

'Oh, thank goodness you are both all right,' their mum said, as they appeared in the kitchen, 'I was worried sick.'

'You don't need to worry about us, Mum,' Mary said. 'We really can look after ourselves, plus we were with Arthur and Gwen, so we couldn't have been any safer.'

'But your dad was attacked when he went to get the bag from the car while you were away. Well, not really attacked. Something that he only glimpsed for a second pulled on his arm as though it wanted him to turn. But then it vanished before he could do anything. He's all right though.'

'There was no harm done,' Bill said. 'Perhaps it was just snooping about and I surprised it. It wasn't a warrior like the others. Well, I don't think it was. To be honest, although I only saw it briefly, it looked very odd. It was virtually translucent and possibly reptilian. I'm not really sure of its size, but I think it was about my height, at least I think that was what I saw.'

Glancing sideways at Mary, David said, 'I wonder what that was?'

His dad just shrugged his shoulders. 'I'm glad you created a safety barrier around the cottage before you left. It certainly helps your mum and me to be able to relax a bit more when there's one in place.'

'Just as long as both of you are all right,' Mary said.

'We are, love,' replied her mum. 'It was you two being out of sight and knowing what had been happening that bothered us.'

'We're fine, Mum, really,' David said. 'In fact, we're more than fine. We're going fishing with Gwen and Arthur after tea, to see if we can improve on our PBs. That's personal bests, Mum, if you didn't know!' Sylvia just smiled. David continued, 'They're coming round here to pick us up about five fifteen, I hope that's all right.'

'No problem, Son.' Sylvia said. 'I'll make sure you both will have had your teas by then.'

'We've all got phones,' Bill said. 'If we need each other, we'll ring. I hope you can all get a new PB, but those big ones you caught last time we fished here were beauties.'

'We decided we'd make it a bit of a competition,' Mary said. 'The pair who don't do well will pay for lunch in Moatcaster tomorrow.'

'So you've both got a date as well,' joked their mum.

'It's not a date, Mum!' They both remarked together. 'It's an outing, just an outing,' David said.

'Still, you need to do things properly,' Sylvia said. 'You had better ask your dad to help you sort out some fishing gear for them to use while I get some tea ready. It wouldn't do for you to be late.' Sylvia and Bill just smiled knowingly at each other.

On the way to the fishing lake, both Arthur and his sister somehow managed to steer the conversation round to whether or not David and Mary had a girlfriend or boyfriend. The expressions on Gwen and Arthur's faces and their body language let their guests see both of them were pleased when it was clear that neither of them did.

The outing was a huge success and they all enjoyed the fishing immensely, despite Arthur almost taking a plunge when a big carp shot off with his bait. Being caught off balance, he stumbled towards the water's edge. Fortunately he managed to regain his balance and save himself from taking a header into the lake which would have been a most embarrassing experience, but it still gave all of them another good and relaxing laugh.

Arthur and Gwen could hardly believe their ears when they were told about the abduction, especially as it was the second time it had happened. They found the story David told them wholly intriguing. But they were both particularly relieved to learn that neither Mary nor David had been harmed in any way by their abductors and all agreed they would like to talk about it on another occasion.

They were particularly pleased with how well the fishing had gone and how much fun and how successful for all of them it had been. They had all improved on their personal bests, each of them having caught a carp weighing almost twenty pounds and they agreed that they were all looking forward to the next fishing trip. They were also particularly happy about and looking forward to the following day's lunch date, as it would give all of them the opportunity to spend more time together.

Back in the cottage, the twins were very happy to tell their parents how they had all improved on their personal bests. Mary, in a particularly happy mood, voiced her view of the evening. 'I have always enjoyed our family fishing sessions, Mum, even the ones with just David.'

'Thanks for that, Sis,' was David's comment.

Mary continued, 'But I think tonight was the most enjoyable fishing session I have ever had.'

'And Arthur and I particularly liked the idea of yours to use Garlic Spam as bait,' Gwen happily remarked. 'We've never used it before and it worked brilliantly. Both of

87

us have thoroughly enjoyed the evening, it's been great, absolutely great! Thank you. Thank you both!'

'There's no need to thank us, Gwen,' David said, 'we both thought it was great as well. We wouldn't have missed it for the world.'

David then closed the discussion with one of his humorous comments. 'We discovered years ago that offering a cube of luncheon meat on a hook caught us a lot of quality carp. It was then we realized how much carp enjoyed a square meal!'

Everyone chuckled.

'It sounds like you've all had an enjoyable and interesting session,' Bill said, 'I wish we had gone with you now, but we didn't want to get in the way,' he added with a wink to Sylvia. 'So, what's on the cards for tomorrow? The weather promises to be good again.'

'You both could have come with us, Dad,' Mary said.

'You would have enjoyed it too,' David said, 'so we'll make sure you are with us next time. As for tomorrow, Arthur and Gwen are coming to pick us up at ten o'clock for a trip into Moatcaster, and perhaps a walk around the castle.' Bill and Sylvia just smiled.

'We agreed the fishing match was a draw, so we'll be buying our own lunch. As we are being picked up, you'll be able to use the car, Dad,' he grinned, 'why not take Mum for a romantic memory lane walk in Moatcaster Castle?'

'We'll see,' Bill said looking a little embarrassed.

'Well, we'll be off now,' Arthur said walking towards the door. 'Thanks for the loan of the tackle, Mister Knight, it served us well. We've both had a great fishing session.'

'Yes, we most certainly have,' Gwen said. 'It's been super. We'll see you all in the morning. Let's hope it's not going to be too eventful a day.'

'Amen to that,' David said as he and Mary walked their new found friends to their car.

'Thanks again for saving us from Offalmire, David and Mary, and it's been a great evening,' Arthur said, and found himself kissing Mary on the cheek. Though oddly she wasn't surprised and he was delighted she didn't pull away.

'And thank you for a great evening and making it so special too,' Mary said, a little nervously but with a big smile. 'I enjoyed every second.' And she grinned broadly.

Gwen had seated herself in the driver's seat while Arthur was saying goodnight and rested her arm in the open window.

Putting his hand on her arm, David leaned into the car and lightly kissed her cheek saying, 'Thank you for a great evening too. Like Mary, I also enjoyed every minute. I am really looking forward to tomorrow. Drive carefully and 'phone me if you have any unwelcome visitors. Mary and I put a shield on your cottage before we left this afternoon, so you should be okay. Try and get a good night's sleep.' And they all waved shouting, 'Goodnight' as they drove away.

David then turned to Mary and said, 'I sense something very special is happening to both of us, Sis, and I like it. I really like it!'

'Me too, David,' Mary replied, 'it's an unusual, though special feeling, isn't it? But I must confess I like it too.'

Holding hands, they turned to walk back into the cottage then stopped dead...Their parents were standing in the open door looking at them with big knowing grins on their faces.

'What! What?'The twins exclaimed in unison. And they all went in. Bill had his arm round Mary and David was being hugged by his mum.

But tomorrow certainly was to be another day, but what sort? Were there to be more problems?

Chapter Ten

MOATCASTER CASTLE RE-VISITED

Everyone enjoyed a really good night's sleep, and secretly wondered if Merlin had made sure they were properly rested after the stressful events of the last couple of days. They all enjoyed sharing breakfast-time together, chatting about the experiences of the last forty eight hours and wondered what they might have to do to get rid of Drossmire.

'I'm glad he's an entity from the Other World and not a real person,' David said, 'or I would be considered a murderer if I killed him.'

'I would be a killer too,' remarked Mary, 'if I was the one to do it or if I helped you.'

'Both of you can stop thinking like that right now,' Bill said, a little anger in his voice. 'He isn't human. He's far from it. He's an evil monster from the black side of magic. He's from the Other World, and an evil being who has no thought for humans at all. Merlin popped in for a chat and a coffee last night when you were fishing, and bent our ears about Drossmire.

'He appears to be like his evil father. He too, delights in hurting or maiming people and considers children to be a delicacy. He frequently goes through time wormholes into parallel worlds to enable him to kidnap them. And I've not even mentioned the horrendous threat of him getting his hands on the Thirteen Treasures of Britain and what he might do if he misuses them. I dread to think what might happen. So please, let's hear no more talk about you possibly feeling a bit guilty, doing so at the wrong time could make you lose your focus. And that could be fatal!

'Believe me, you will be doing the whole world a service when you rid it of the threat of Drossmire's presence.'

'Your dad's absolutely right,' Sylvia said. 'So if you ever feel you need to reproach yourself just remember why you are the Terrestrial Twins. The Gods of the Terrestrial Light bestowed their powers on you for the good of man, to redress any threats from the Other World or even evil criminals in our world, and that's all you really need to remember. What you have or need to do with them will come naturally as your actions are guided by the forces of good. And in any case, everything you do will be in a supernaturally created parallel time, not our time. So go and get the pots washed and let's all enjoy the day.'

David and Mary both laughed at their mum's last remark and headed for the kitchen with the tray of pots.

'Oh, and enjoy your new friendships,' Sylvia continued, 'you all looked so happy together. You both looked so pleased that Arthur and Gwen just popped into your lives.'

But not a word came out of the kitchen until the pots were washed and put away.

'Sis and I have been talking,' David said as they re-entered the lounge, 'and we would like you both to come with us into Moatcaster this morning.'

'Yes,' Mary said, 'as much as we enjoyed being with Arthur and Gwen on our own yesterday, we can't help but worry that on your own you're are easy targets, so we would be happier if you said yes to coming with us. There will be plenty of time after Drossmire has gone to get to know them better, so for now, and as the Terrestrial Twins, not just your twins, we feel it is best that we all stay together. And let's not lose sight of the fact either that we are supposed to be on a *family* holiday.'

'Arthur and Gwen won't be here for at least half an hour,' David said, 'so you have plenty of time to get ready. And we don't want to hear any excuses.'

Their parents just looked at each other and grinned. 'Wow, he sounded just like you, Bill, ' Sylvia said almost laughing, as she and Bill went obediently to their room to get ready.

This time when they left the cottage, no one was wearing the Magpies strip which they were all particularly proud of, but they were all still wearing their bum bags, as they had become part of their daily wardrobe since their last Castershire trip. It was a hot day so they only needed light tops, shorts and trainers. Mary had opted for a pale blue vest and white shorts. Her mum wore a similar dark green top with paler green shorts. David was sporting a pale green polo shirt and dark green shorts. Bill was all in black.

After David had explained to Arthur and Gwen why their parents were accompanying them, they agreed that it was a sensible idea, and as there was more room in the Knight's car they all climbed in and set off for Moatcaster.

Gwen had opted to wear a white polo shirt and shorts to match. Arthur was looking as relaxed and comfortable as everyone else in a khaki vest and dark green shorts. Bill chose to drive so the twins could all sit together and they set off for town a little after 10.00 a.m. They had been travelling for a little over ten minutes when Bill commented about a huge black truck that was gradually getting closer and closer to their rear bumper.

'It might be them, Dad,' David said, having turned to have a look. 'Isn't that long narrow bridge near Tinker's Hall just ahead?'

'Yes, Son,' Bill replied, 'have you got an idea?'

'Yes, Dad, but it won't work until we get there. So you'll have to put up with him threatening us. Are you going to be okay?'

'I'll cope,' Bill replied, 'I'll just treat him as a stupid road hog.'

'If the driver is one of Drossmire's men,' David joked, trying to lighten the obvious tension building in the car, 'it could very well be a hog!'

Finally, after being closely and dangerously shadowed and almost bumped by the huge truck for a couple of miles or so, they started descending the hill towards the river. At the bottom of the hill was the narrow, though quite long, virtually flat bridge over the river, which was controlled by traffic lights, a set at both ends. Fortunately, as they approached the lights turned in their favour.

David was about to say something to his father as he reached for Mary's hand. But before he was able to finish what he had planned to say, he and everyone else in the car gasped as a builder's truck waiting on the other side of the bridge, ignored the red light facing it and continued at speed towards them. The huge vehicle closing behind them was now also picking up speed.

'That builder's truck has got scaffolding poles protruding towards us over the cab,' David yelled. 'It intends to squash and probably decapitate us between it and the lorry!'

He grabbed Mary's hand, muttered something, and their car disappeared.

A huge crashing and almost deafening explosion almost instantly followed as the two vehicles which had been virtually hurtling towards each other from opposite directions, inevitably smashed into each other on the bridge and exploded on impact. Within seconds of the explosion both vehicles suddenly disappeared, leaving no trace of what had just happened.

After the two vehicles disappeared, the Knight's car rematerialized in the Tinker's Hall car park which was only a couple of hundred yards beyond the bridge.

'We were very lucky that time,' David said. 'It's obvious Drossmire doesn't want us around any longer. We'll all have to be really careful from now on.'

'I thought we all had been,' his mum said, 'it's not possible to anticipate things like that, Son, is it? Anyway, what was it you were going to say before you did what you did?'

Everyone laughed at that, which was a good thing, as they had all been really frightened and shaken up by the bridge incident.

'I was about to tell Dad to turn right into the little side road just before the bridge. The lorry wouldn't have been able to have made the turn at that speed, so we would have been able to avoid him running into us. But the builder's truck setting off and heading towards us distracted me.' He then joked, 'I'm sure I can smell bacon or roast pork. Can't you?' Everyone smiled.

Continuing on their journey towards Moatcaster, they were all surprised to learn that Arthur and Gwen had moved a little over two years ago to live in Pullister, which was only about twenty miles from where the Knight family lived in Oxtown. Apparently Arthur and Gwen had been born and spent the first twelve years of their lives in Nodcaster before moving to Bullinsfield to suit their fathers' occupation. David also thought it a little odd that their surname was Dey, as it meant their developing friendship linked their names as Knight and Dey. How strange was that?

Having found a place to park in the car park opposite the castle, Mary suggested they all should visit it again to have a good look round together. So they did.

'Perhaps we could introduce Gwen and Arthur to Red?' David said as they entered the castle's grassed central area. 'He's a great character, literally. You'll really like him! I think this place is absolutely brillfanmagical. Don't you think so?'

Gwen, with a big grin on her face replied, 'Yes, it is, David. There's something very special about it. Can't you feel it, Arthur?'

'Yes. Yes I can. I can't explain it, but yes, I agree with David's word. It is a brillfanmagical place.' They all laughed at Arthur using one of David's favourite words.

'Does Red work here?' enquired Gwen, picking up on David's earlier comment.

'You could say that,' replied David. 'Part of his job is to guard, so yes, he works here. We'll see if he's in and take you to meet him.'

'Will they be able to do that?' questioned Sylvia.

'Unless he's invisible, I should think we might be able to see him,' replied Arthur, his comment bringing a laugh this time from all the Knight family.

'What did I say that was so funny?' Arthur asked with a puzzled smile on his face.

'You'll see in a minute or two,' replied Bill. 'He's up there in the King's Banqueting Hall. We'll all go up now and have a chat with him, he'll like that.'

They all stopped for a moment when they were about two thirds of the way up the stairs, and Sylvia, with a grin on her face, turned to Gwen and Arthur.

'Firstly, you will see even in the dim light how huge the hall is and that it appears to be empty.' They then continued up and emerged through the arch at the top of the stairs into the hall. 'As I said on the way up, it's a huge room which appears to be empty, but I can assure you it isn't.'

'You were certainly right about it being big,' Gwen said, 'but apart from that table, it does appear to be empty.'

'We realize it does look empty,' Sylvia said, 'but this banqueting hall is really where Red actually resides. We laughed earlier because you said unless he was invisible you would be able to see him.'

'You mean he really is invisible then?' Arthur said with disbelief in his voice.

'Yes, he really is, and you will shortly appreciate why,' David said.

'That's a bit difficult, David. How can they see why if he's invisible,' Mary joked.

Then seemingly talking into thin air, David said, 'Hello, Red, we're back in Castershire and we've brought a couple of friends with us today to meet you.'

Then, out of the seemingly empty cavern, came what was to them a deep friendly and familiar voice which echoed all round the huge room.

'Good morning, David and Mary, and of course your lovely parents, I hope the twins have been looking after you properly, Sylvia and Bill. It really is so good to see you all looking so well.'

'Where is he, I can't see him?' Gwen whispered into David's ear.

'I'm here, but like all the others who come in here you are unable to see me,' Red said, having heard her whispered question. 'I understand and am fully aware that most ordinary humans would find me... I think the phrase is, a bit scary, so most of the time I remain invisible. But, if you promise not to be too scared, nothing would please me more than to become visible for a short time. Prepare yourself for a bit of a shock.'

Then both Arthur and Gwen gasped. Gwen, putting her hand to her mouth as she almost screamed out loud as she and Arthur instinctively took a step back. For there, not too many feet away from them, had appeared a splendid, bus sized, fully scaled red dragon. A proper live dragon!

'Now you can see how handsome I am,' Red said.

'Wow!' Arthur and Gwen said together.

'And you're right,' Gwen said, 'you really are handsome, Red. I think you are wonderful.'

'Thank you, Gwen for that very polite remark. It's good to see you and your brother Arthur have at last met up with the Knight family.'

'You know who we are then?' Arthur said.

'Oh yes, Arthur, I've known you all since you were babies, even Bill and Sylvia. I have always been a part of all the mythological plans. Merlin has always kept me informed of what was happening, and I have kept an eye on things for him in the region and particularly here.'

'I'll explain that later,' David said, 'as we see more of the castle.'

As they could hear someone else coming up the steps to the King's Banqueting Hall, and with a bright, 'Cheerio!' to everyone, Red returned to his usual invisible self.

It was now time to see more of the brillfanmagical Moatcaster Castle...

Chapter Eleven

MERLIN'S INVISIBLE CRYSTAL TOWER

'It was here in the castle grounds that the main action, and mammoth sized and at times savage battle, took place two years ago,' Bill said, as they walked nearer the King's Tower in the centre of the Moatcaster Castle complex. 'It was an awesome experience which none of us will ever forget. Let's hope we don't ever have another one like it.'

'It really is an amazing building,' Sylvia said. 'What's that word you use, David?'

'Brillfanmagical, Mum,' David replied with a big smile on his face. 'Brillfanmagical!'

'And you're right too,' Arthur said. 'Gwen and I felt it as soon as we walked in. You can sense there is something, something very special about it.'

'We've all felt it,' Mary said, 'and just there, where that patch of grass is slightly more yellow, is where Drossmire's father King Offalmire died.'

'And from there Drossmire absorbed from underground some of his father's strengths and powers,' Bill said.

'Let's all go into the King's Tower,' Sylvia said, as she walked towards the door. 'Are you sensing any bad vibes, kids?' she asked, addressing David and Mary.

'No, Mum, none at all, it's all clear,' replied Mary. So they all went in.

Then, surprisingly, and this time witnessed by everyone, the whispery figure of an old lady dressed in a simple white cotton, full length smock appeared in a shaft of golden light. Then pointing at David and Mary said, 'I warned you last time you were in here two years ago about witches and water. I now feel I need to again warn you. Beware of water and the threat of evil beings wherever you go.' Then, as before, she faded and was gone.

'Did you see her two years ago?' Sylvia asked, sounding a little surprised.

'Yes, Mum,' replied Mary, 'but we didn't tell you in case you became more nervous than you already were.'

'And do you think I'm not nervous now then?' she replied. 'I can assure you, I unfortunately am. That visitor and her repeated warning did nothing at all to relax me.'

'Don't upset yourself, love,' Bill said, reaching to take hold of his wife's hand. 'I am confident that together we are quite a formidable team. Providing we keep our minds alert and use our commonsense as to what we do and where we go, we should be all right. And don't forget, love, there are six of us now, last time there was only four.'

'Don't forget Sir Gawain and Mabel, Dad,' Mary said a big smile on her face. And turning to Arthur and Gwen went on to say, 'We'll tell you about them another time.'

David interrupted them. 'I agree with what Dad said. We're a much stronger team now, so if we continue to stay alert we'll be fine.'

David then went on to tell Arthur and Mary about the invisible crystal tower created by Merlin centuries ago, which he had magically hidden along with its special supernatural contents in the very building in which they were standing, the King's Tower. And it was the invisible crystal tower which up to now had prevented Drossmire from reaching the special supernatural Treasures.

However, Merlin had now sadly informed them that sometime in the next few days Drossmire's magic would become powerful enough to be able to get into the Treasures. Part of their job was to ensure he didn't.

David then went on to remind everyone that they would have to get in touch with Merlin soon if they were to find out what his plans were. 'At the moment we have no idea what he has in mind and time is moving on,' he said. 'We really could do with being told.'

Merlin then made everyone jump when he suddenly materialized behind them saying, 'You are quite right, David, time is moving on and we do need to discuss what needs to be done and how we might proceed.'

'I wish you wouldn't do that, Merlin,' Bill joked, 'creeping up on us like that. We're all a bit on edge at the moment you know.'

'Yes, you all must be, I am sorry. I'm glad to see you all though and wanted to take this opportunity to let you in on my plans.'

Mary looked around furtively.

'Don't worry, Mary,' continued Merlin. 'We're quite safe talking here. Although you don't realize it, you're actually standing very close to my crystal tower. Even though it isn't visible, its supernatural properties are currently surrounding us and will keep this conversation just between ourselves.'

Merlin waited a moment. Although they all knew the crystal tower was invisible, the Knight family and their new friends couldn't help but look around for traces of its magical existence. Merlin smiled in a fatherly sort of way before beginning to explain his plan.

'I have already spoken of Drossmire's formidable cunning and abilities, and of me not being able to clearly penetrate his thinking. Well, I have managed to infiltrate his organization by using one of his henchmen. I lured him into my badger sett, having first cast a spell on him. I told him of my plans with you, knowing he would feed them back to Drossmire. And he did.'

'Are you going to keep it a secret from us then?' David jokingly asked.

Merlin laughed, 'No, David, of course not, and some of it could even be fun.'

'Fun, Merlin!, Fun! How can trying to stay alive while trying to kill Drossmire be classed as fun?' Sylvia blurted out.

Bill, putting his arms round his wife, lovingly pulled her to him. 'Steady, love. I am sure Merlin has a good reason for saying what he did, but I can understand where you are coming from. Fun hardly seems the right word, Merlin.'

'Forgive me for upsetting you, Sylvia, that was not my intention. Please allow me to explain more fully.'

'The message I implanted in the brain of Drossmire's goblin, was that you had all decided to visit Tinker's Hall in three days' time to re-enact some of the jousting and fighting events that took place there centuries ago, just to have a bit of fun. This I am certain will be of great interest to Drossmire, as I am told he likes nothing better than being entertained by contests and hand-to-hand combat, even though he is a born coward himself. Such an event will be too much for him to ignore, and so should present you with an opportunity to rid the world of him. That is what I meant by "it could also be fun", the first part of the plan that is, not the last.'

Bill was now holding Sylvia's hand and they noticed the twins were holding hands too, but in a way that brought a smile to their parents' faces. For some reason David, standing close to Gwen, was holding her hand. Arthur, close to Mary, was holding hers.

'That's a heck of an idea,' Bill said, addressing Merlin. 'It will probably work too, and you could also be right that it might be fun. I really believe it could be. What do you think about it, David?'

'I'm sorry you were upset, Mum, and I understand why, but it feels all right to me. It should give us a number of opportunities to do what we know has to be done.' He let go of Gwen's hand to hold his sister's, who had moved closer to him. 'Yes, it could and should work.'

'Yes, it should,' Mary added. 'I can understand Merlin's thinking and yes, I agree. It's a good plan and much of it, as you say, could be a lot of fun too. Let's do it.'

'But don't underestimate Drossmire,' Sylvia said, 'he's very devious. We only have one life, let's not throw it away.'

With that, Merlin said his goodbyes and faded, saying he would be around if needed. They all left the castle walking in pairs and holding hands to enjoy a peaceful stroll by the river where the swans were.

'I hope you don't mind me asking,' Bill said, addressing Arthur and Gwen, 'but which of your parents has black hair?'

Arthur replied, 'Our dad, like you Mister Knight. Mum has almost white hair, very much like Missus Knight's.'

'What's that building down there?' David asked, pointing a little way ahead of them.

'I believe that's part of the old gatehouse. Part of the medieval south east end of Moatcaster's defensive wall,' Bill replied. 'If I remember correctly, it was a four storey tower that used to have a drawbridge across the river, but I can't remember what it's called.'

'This footpath by the river certainly makes a pleasant place to walk with all those water birds swimming about,' Sylvia added, 'especially on a day as nice as today.'

'Will we be able to have a look in that building?' Arthur asked. 'It looks such an interesting place.'

Both Arthur and Gwen then voiced their disappointment when having reached the building they discovered that the steel barred gate was locked.

'There may be a way in,' David said, squeezing Gwen's hand a little more tightly. 'You keep a good grip on Arthur's hand, Sis, and we'll see if we can walk through. We'll only be a minute, Mum, Dad. We hope you don't mind waiting?'

'No, Son,' Bill replied. 'We'll be all right out here, we'll sit on this bench until you come out, but don't be too long.'

David then took hold of Mary's free hand with his and walked up to the barred gate. He then quickly explained to Arthur and Gwen that he and Mary would walk them through the closed bars and into the building.

It was obvious from the looks of total disbelief on Arthur and Gwen's faces that they doubted it was possible. Nevertheless, the events of the last few days had shown them that so much they previously thought unbelievable was actually very real. They had been kidnapped by an evil king from another world and held prisoner in a castle dungeon with a real live wizard before magically escaping; they'd seen goblins melt into gooey heaps of sticky mucus, met an invisible dragon and seen a suspicious old lady give out an eerie warning. How unbelievable could it be to walk through a locked gate? Holding hands confidently with David and Mary they stepped towards and magically through the bars and into the ground floor of the old stone building.

'I bet that's a first for you two,' David said.

'Yes,' Arthur and Gwen said together.

'And it didn't hurt, thank goodness,' Arthur said. 'Now I begin to see just what kind of abilities you two have been blessed with. We really did miss out, didn't we, Gwen?'

'Remember, we didn't choose to have any of them,' Mary said. 'The Gods of the Terrestrial Light blessed us as the Terrestrial Twins. Seemingly it had been and still is our mythological destiny.'

'What we must never do,' David said, 'is misuse our powers, and while I'm thinking about it, I think what we just did was taking things as far as we ever should. The special abilities we have been blessed with are for protecting terrestrial beings, mainly human beings. They are not for us to abuse or use willy nilly.'

'I sense an entity has just arrived close by somewhere,' Mary said. 'I think we should go back outside and make sure Mum and Dad are both all right.'

David agreed, and after having a brief glance around the room they were in, they returned the way they had come and walked through the barred door out on to the grass pathway.

Bill was smiling as he spoke to Arthur and Gwen saying, 'That was a bit different wasn't it? They did that to us in a cave on the way here. It gave both me and their mum the heebie-jeebies I can tell you.'

Arthur laughingly said, 'I think that's what it did to us too. It really is a different experience and one which I somehow doubt we are ever likely to forget in a hurry.'

'Do you still detect a goblin or something, Sis?' David asked. 'I did in there, but I don't feel it now.'

'No, Bruv, I don't either,' Mary said. 'Perhaps it was a flying one and it's now passed by.'

'Do you think it might have been just one of those water birds, just swanning about?' David jokingly said. Everyone smiled and nodded.

'I fancied some fish and chips earlier,' David said, 'but as it's so warm, I think I now prefer a ham salad or something. What do you fancy, Gwen?'

'A ham salad sounds a good idea, David. I think I could enjoy one too.'

Everyone got the message. It was time to find somewhere for lunch.

'We know just the place,' Sylvia said.

And off they went for something to eat. En route David said, 'What's worse than finding a caterpillar in the salad you are enjoying eating?'

And Gwen fell for it saying, 'I don't know. What is worse than finding a caterpillar in your salad, David?'

David laughingly replied, 'Finding only half of one!'

They all smiled again and kept walking.

Chapter Twelve

BUZZED ON THE BEACH

As it was still a really hot and lovely, sunny day when they returned to their car after enjoying lunch, Bill suggested they all revisit Serpent Dunes Sands beach. But this time David and Mary would first create a safety barrier around their car. They didn't want to risk any chance of a repetition of the terrifying experience they had two years ago, when they literally had a *flying visit*.

Speaking to Arthur and Gwen, Sylvia asked if they had ever done any surfing.

'We have done quite a bit actually,' was Gwen's reply. 'In fact Arthur is particularly good at it and Mum and Dad and his friends at work have tried to get him to compete, but he won't. He says he would rather just enjoy it and compete with the water.' Then, addressing David and Mary, she asked, 'Do you two surf?'

'We used to,' David answered, 'but we discovered we lose far too much of our special abilities when we are wet, so we always have to bear that in mind. That was what the warning from the old lady was all about when we were in the King's Tower this morning. We have to stay dry and keep out of water, particularly while we are here in Castershire. But there is no reason why you two shouldn't enjoy yourselves if you fancy going surfing.'

'David's right,' Bill said, 'we can hire some suits and boards, then you two can go into the sea and have some fun. I mentioned we were going to Serpent Dunes Sands beach, and that's a very popular surfing beach. Do you know it?'

'Gwen and I were taken by surprise when you said it as it's our favourite beach,' Arthur replied, 'we've spent many happy hours surfing there.'

'That's it then,' Sylvia said, I've got towels and a hair brush and comb in the car, all you need is the gear.'

'And I know where to get that,' Bill said, 'so we'll go and hire some for you now. We can enjoy watching you while we walk on the beach or in the sand dunes. That beach is one of our favourite places too.'

It had been noon when they went for lunch, so they had the whole afternoon to enjoy the Serpent Dunes Sands beach.

Having used the toilet block at the beach car park in which to get changed, the Knight family accompanied Arthur and Gwen to the water's edge. As the tide was coming in, they went a little further north up the beach, away from the rocks where they had met the sand witch two years earlier.

It was very obvious from the way they performed that both Arthur and Gwen were very happy on surf boards and they were both really accomplished surfers.

It was a joy to watch their range of take-offs, exciting pivots and expert variety of changes in direction. Arthur's 360° stalling manoeuvres and his lifting off the water to become airborne brought a round of enthusiastic applause from everyone on the beach.

'Aren't they good?' Sylvia remarked. 'It's a pity you two can't enjoy it with them, but I do understand your need for caution.'

'We can surf with them another time, Mum. But not here and now, it's too risky,' David said, 'but yes, they are very good.'

'Particularly Arthur,' Mary said, a noticeable note of admiration in her voice, 'and doesn't he look manly in that wet suit?' she added, a big grin on her face.

'Gwen has my vote,' David said, 'I think she looks…' he paused, 'very feminine.'

'That's enough, you two,' Bill said with a knowing grin on his face. 'You're fair drooling over them. Let's leave it at that and say they both look good, shall we?'.

He had just finished speaking, when a fully helmeted rider in a brown one-piece suit driving a dark brown quad bike came shooting out of the sand dunes and roared between them forcing them all to leap sideways to avoid being run down and killed. It became painfully obvious that the driver meant to do them harm, when, having turned, he brought the vehicle tearing back again and headed straight at the twins.

'We can't zap him,' David shouted as he leapt clear of the churning wheels. 'Some of the other people on the beach who are watching the surfing have noticed what is happening. They can see we're being buzzed and are now watching to see what might happen next.'

It was Mary's turn to dive from the next attack, shouting as she plunged headlong into the sand. 'We were warned again to expect trouble near water!'

'What if it goes for Mum and Dad?' she yelled as she jumped quickly back to her feet.

David replied, yelling, 'FOLLOW ME, SIS!' And he ran up to the head of the beach and into the sand dunes with Mary hot on his heels. But it was really difficult trying to run in the soft sand and they only just made it. They were both forced yet again to leap to one side as the quad bike came roaring at them, each of them skillfully avoiding being knocked flying and killed.

Then David, standing on a tuft of greenery on the side of a dune, called to Mary. 'The people on the beach can't see us now. Wave your hands about, Sis and entice him to run at you. I'll get him as he comes past.'

Having turned, the quad bike came roaring back, again attempting to flatten Mary who now looked an easy target. But as it came alongside him David threw himself in a well-aimed drop kick, hitting his target on the head and shoulders and knocking him flying off the bike.

Both twins, without giving him a chance to get up, pointed their forefingers at him and with thin bolts of lightning shooting out, together they zapped him. The rider shuddered and after giving a low squeal melted into a green and brown pool of ooze, over which the twins liberally kicked sand. The quad bike disappeared into thin air as they did.

On returning to where their parents were anxiously standing holding hands, they shouted to the curious onlookers that the quad bike had gone and that they were both all right.

'That was another close call,' Bill said. 'Drossmire's not giving up easily is he?'

'As long as you two are all right,' Sylvia said. 'I was really worried that time.'

By this time, Arthur and Gwen, having seen David and Mary running into the dunes, had left the fun they were enjoying in the surf and joined them.

'Are you all right?' they both asked.

'Yes, we're both fine thanks,' David replied. 'It will take someone or something better than that brown clad moron to floor me and Sis.'

'Let's get you two back and changed out of those wet suits,' Sylvia said.

'Don't be a spoilsport, Mum. You know Mary was admiring Arthur in his.'

'And what about you having a good look at Gwen in hers?' Mary replied.

'Come on you two. Grow up!' Bill said.

'I'm not going to reply to that comment, Dad,' David joked as they headed back to the car park changing rooms.

'You two were brilliant on those surf boards,' David said when they returned to the car after changing. 'Gwen was right, Arthur you are definitely up to competition standard. You were a pleasure to watch. And you're pretty good too, Gwen! We have to agree don't we, Sis, they're both better than us.'

'I've never been able to stall and turn like you did, Arthur. You'll have to teach me sometime.'

'It will be my pleasure,' replied Arthur, 'but are you sure you're both all right after that quad attack?'

'Were both fine thanks, honest,' David said, but it could have been much worse, but now to change the subject. How about all of us going for another spot of carp fishing after tea, and that means you too, Mum and Dad? We're not leaving you behind this time, especially as Drossmire's entities are becoming so active. It's not worth the risk.'

'Okay then, that's settled,' David said. 'And the losing team buys fish and chips on the way home.'

They all agreed that it sounded a good idea and settled down to chatting on the way back about all that had happened, both the morning's events and the afternoon's surfing and the quad bike incident. But also hoping there would be no more unwanted visits or events... at least not today.

Chapter Thirteen

A SWARM OF STINGERS

During tea and whilst everyone enjoyed the scrambled eggs Sylvia had cooked, followed by the delicious individual trifles she had stored in the fridge, conversation turned to driving. Bill had started to say that when he was being taught to drive, he was told to consider that he had an imaginary nervous old lady passenger in the back seat holding a basket of eggs on her lap and a glass of water in her hand.

But before he could finish speaking, David interrupted and started to finish the story, saying the idea was not to frighten the old lady. Mary then, having interrupted David, went on to finish what both her dad and David had been saying with, 'And also to always brake steadily so as to not frighten the old lady, not spill the water or crack any of the eggs!'

Arthur then joined in and began to recall what his driving instructor had said. 'Drivers who are impatient drivers...' he began.

Gwen butted-in to finish the phrase, 'Only too often become in-patient drivers.'

Sylvia added words of wisdom from her driving instructor. 'It is better to arrive alive, than to be dead on time.'

Continuing to chat about their instructor's entertaining driving lessons, they all had a good laugh when it suddenly become very obvious that they had all, although many years and places apart, been taught to drive, by the same driving instructor, called Alan. Was this another supernatural coincidence?

Apparently it had been snowing for a few days when Gwen had taken one of her lessons and she could remember there had been a lot of accidents reported in the local press and on TV. Alan had said that it was mainly because too many drivers failed to adjust their speed and the way they used their brakes, and because they failed to leave a wider gap between vehicles in such conditions. He had gone on to tell her that many drivers ignored the basic simple rule of good driving by failing to drive their car to suit the change in surface conditions. 'You can't drive as normal in conditions that aren't,' he'd repeatedly said. 'Too many drivers fail to be aware that anything on the road surface, no matter what it is, means the car's tyres can't grip or are possibly not even touching the road surface, because they can't. Whether it is because of mud, sand, oil, leaves, ice or snow, the effect is the same. All of these and more can and do negatively affect braking, speed and steering and any driver ignoring these facts does so at their own peril. Too many drivers, sadly far too many young drivers, fail to accept the responsibility that it's not the car that does the killing, it's the driver.'

Gwen went on to say that she had been so impressed with his commonsense and wise words, that she could even remember the limerick poem he submitted to a local paper.

A young driver whose name we don't know,
Went out for a drive in the snow,
But instead of slowing, he just kept going,
They cremate him tomorrow you know.

After tea they loaded their gear and set off for the fishery. As Arthur and Gwen didn't have their tackle with them, they decided to fish in pairs, David with Gwen and Mary with Arthur. Their mum and dad fished together as usual.

It was a beautiful, warm and calm evening. The birds were singing and butterflies were flitting and gliding about. The three couples were enjoying being in their partner's company and they had the lake to themselves as no one else was fishing. It seemed an almost perfect end to a mostly wonderful day.

They had only been fishing for about ten minutes when a strange, deep, droning sound, steadily increasing in volume, broke the calm and pleasant evening. From the far end of the lake a

strange dark cloud began to build and to slowly descend as it approached them.

Bill and Sylvia were the nearest to it and were the first to realize what it was. And with a noticeable tone of terror in his voice Bill loudly yelled, 'WASPS! A HUGE SWARM OF RUDDY WASPS!'

As they slowly drew nearer the terrifying drone got louder and louder. David jumped up, and with a couple of swirls of his forefinger, he magically created a fine mesh net over his parents. Mary did the same over Arthur and herself. David then repeated the supernatural action and created a protective net over Gwen and himself.

The awesome droning sound continued to increase in volume slowly and steadily until it reached an horrendous and frightening intensity, obliterating all other sounds. The mass of evil buzzing, virtually throbbing sound, of the awesome evil insects, their stings protruding threateningly from their abdomens, smothered the whole area like a horrible heaving yellow and black blanket. It was an unbelievably hideous and terrifying sight.

Unfortunately, the fishing rods were still protruding from under the protective nets enabling some of the cleverer wasps to crawl along them and get inside the safety net. Once inside, their bodies swelled to almost a foot in size before they viciously attacked and attempted to sting the occupants.

Both David and Mary were able to zap them when they crawled under their nets, but they realized their parents would be in real trouble.

'This is a bit too much for us to cope with, Sis,' David rather tensely said, 'we had better ask the Terrestrial Light Gods to help us.' He raised his voice so that Mary could hear him above the droning and buzzing of the evil wasps, and sensibly also mentally communicated with her just to be sure.

'Good idea, Bruv, ready when you are.'

Twinning by telepathy they linked their thoughts and loudly said in unison, 'Please, Gods of the Terrestrial Light, please help us rid ourselves of these evil insects.'

There was a blinding flash like a huge photographic flashbulb going off, and the droning and buzzing instantly ceased as the yellow and black heaving horror blanket of wasps thankfully disappeared.

David and Mary, having thanked the Gods, removed the safety nets from everyone and they all gathered together to talk, removing their baited hooks from the water as they did.

'Are you all right, Mum?' David asked. 'That was a terrifying experience. A bit more than an anxious moment I think.'

'Yes, thank you, Son,' Sylvia replied. 'I'm a bit shaky, but apart from that I'm Okay. Really! Fortunately neither of us got stung. We came close a few times, but your Dad came to the rescue.'

'Was anybody stung?' Bill asked.

'No, I don't think so,' Mary replied, 'but like you, we almost were.'

'That was an horrendous experience,' Arthur said, 'and not a situation I would ever like to find myself in again. We would like to thank the Terrestrial Light Gods for getting rid of them. Without theirs and David and Mary's help, we would all have been stung to death.'

'I think that was Drossmire's plan,' David said. 'Nothing like that could have happened naturally. It was definitely a contrived, supernatural incident, created to hopefully kill all of us. We are lucky to be the Terrestrial Twins, or we wouldn't be standing around like this talking about it.'

'Let's go back to our rods and try and catch some fish,' Mary said, changing the subject. 'That's what we came to do, and as nobody has caught anything yet and there's almost two hours of the evening left, let's get our Spam back in the water and see if we can catch a monster!'

'Did you have to use that word?' Sylvia said. 'I've had more than enough of monsters for today thank you very much!'

David's next comment only raised a little smile from everyone. Trying to lighten the mood, he said, 'I never thought we'd get buzzed twice in one day.'

David waited for his parents to return to their fishing place to cast in and resume fishing, before he and Gwen walked over to where Mary and Arthur were settling down, hoping for a decent sized carp. They had something on their minds and wanted to talk about it…

Chapter Fourteen

ALIEN ABDUCTIONS

When David and Gwen arrived at the spot where Arthur and Mary were fishing David said, 'I thought, as this seemed a good time and place for it, Mary and I felt we would have a word with you about our abduction.'

'Yes, you're right, great minds think alike, Bruv,' Mary said, 'I was hoping we might all have a chat about it at sometime this evening. Firstly though,' she said addressing Arthur and Gwen, 'do you two believe in flying saucers and extraterrestrials? David and I and our mum and dad do.'

Arthur spoke first. 'Yes, we most certainly do. That's all our family I mean.'

'But Mum's not totally happy about the idea of being abducted. She considers it is an intrusion on her privacy, and I suppose it is. But she does believe in extraterrestrials. She says it would be naïve of us to think Earth was the only planet of the hundreds of billions of stars and things that are out there that might support life. Even if it might not be life as we know it. She says we call them aliens because they really are alien to human beings.'

Gwen then added, 'And Dad's always going on about them.'

'Yes,' Arthur said, 'whenever he sees or reads of anyone even mentioning any sort of UFO incident, or anyone saying they have had a close encounter, he draws our attention to the article or bulletin referring to it.'

Gwen butted in with, 'I think there is something in his job that's related to such things, but as he never really discusses his work, it's just a feeling Arthur and I share.'

'That's great then,' Mary said. 'David and I were hoping we were all, shall I say, together in our thinking on this subject? Or, as Dad would say, "all singing from the same hymn sheet," as it will make our conversations much more compatible.'

'Yes,' David said, 'it would have been really difficult if we had needed to first try to convince you that such things are possible, in some instances real, and in our case very real.'

Arthur then really surprised David and Mary when he said, 'We didn't mention it to either of you earlier for, like you, we were also waiting for the right moment. But as you two had been, Gwen and I were also abducted. But it was two years ago.'

There was a brief pause for a second or two while Mary and David thought about the remarkable statement Arthur had just made.

Mary then came in with, 'Were you fully aware of what was happening to you, Gwen?'

'A lot of the time, yes, but like you two they didn't hurt either of us.'

'It happened to us two years ago, as I said,' continued Arthur, 'when we were sixteen and here in Castershire providing possible support for you when you became the Terrestrial Twins on your fifteenth birthday. We told our parents about it, but nothing has happened since then. Well, nothing of which we are aware.'

'Did you see them?' Mary asked. 'What did they look like? I think, if my clouded memory is now serving me correctly, as I have been giving it an awful lot of thought,

I think the last time it happened to us there were two different kinds of extraterrestrial abductors. One was very humanoid, the other similar but slightly reptilian.'

'It's odd that you have managed to recall those images, Sis,' David said, 'as I too have been racking my brain hoping to remember, and I now realize that what you have just described are the same images that I managed to remember.'

'I couldn't really see much detail of who abducted us because of the brightness of the lights,' Gwen said, 'but I would say the figures you just described, Mary, were the same as those I have in the back of my mind.'

'And I'll go along with that too,' Arthur said. 'We think your description is just about spot on.'

'So we, Mary and I,' David said, 'have seemingly been abducted by two separate and different forms of entities. Two different types of extraterrestrials, as the first lot were more like the "greys" we read about. So it looks like we are of interest and importance to both lots.'

'I think we were beamed up into some sort of spacecraft the last time,' Mary said, 'that's why we now realize our abductors were different from the first lot two years ago in Lilymire Grotto. It could be they are a group who exist in the labyrinth of caves.'

'I second that, Sis,' David said. 'It looks like we all are becoming popular,' he joked.

'Was there a structure on top of that Lilymire Grotto building?' Arthur asked, 'something or some sort of area which might conceivably be considered as a UFO landing pad?'

After a second or two's thought, David replied, 'Yes, there was! To be honest I hadn't thought about it until you just mentioned it, but yes, there was a flat, oblong shaped raised platform, something like about fifty feet across by about seventy or eighty feet long. It's above the building and set back about fifty feet from the edge.'

'And was there a structure attached to it on its rear edge that makes it look like the handle of an oblong ping-pong or table tennis bat or paddle?' Gwen asked, which brought a big smile to David's face.

'Yes, there was, and is, love,' David replied, 'and I couldn't have put it better.'

'In that case,' Arthur said, 'that's probably where the portal into and out of the alien's section of the grotto is situated. That at any rate is according to one of Dad's theories, as he has visited a number of sites in various parts of the world that have similar structures. That much we do know as he has spoken about them.'

'And I can see it being right,' Mary said. 'It makes so much sense.'

'There are ufologists all over the world,' David said, 'who are firmly convinced that similar structures on the top of a variety of buildings created around one to six thousand years ago, or even much earlier, are possibly UFO pads, particularly those on Inca, Aztec, Maya and Chinese structures, and on a variety of pyramids in Egypt and other parts of the world.'

'In fact, I spotted some interesting details when surfing the net just before we came on holiday. I came across some fascinating information on a number of web sites when I was looking at some UFO stuff. Apparently, and for some top secret reason, the US Air Force have unbelievably actually built a huge pyramid on their Nevada base known as Area 51. And I'm sure there will be an awful lot of people all over the world who would like to know why, especially as it has a flattened top. Why would they go to such lengths and such expense to construct such a thing?'

'That's a new one on me,' Arthur said, 'Dad's never mentioned that one.'

'It can be seen on a number of web sites by anybody who bothers to look,' Mary said. 'There obviously isn't loads of information, but there are a number of different web pages showing various satellite images. In fact there is also a large, flat-topped, circular raised area not far from the pyramid. Along with many other people, David and I also wondered about the reason for it being there and for what purpose might it be used.'

'We'll have to talk to Dad and see what, if anything, he might know,' Gwen said.

'And we'll have a look at it on the net sometime,' Arthur said, 'it all sounds very mysterious and interesting. Have you any theories, David, or do you think it's a sort of watch this space situation?'

'I think that's exactly what it is,' David replied, 'I very much doubt the US Air Force are likely to inform the world at large about it in the foreseeable near future, especially as it all seems so relatively new. Anyway, everything that happens at Area 51 seems to have a Top Secret label on it.

'However, there is one question I would really like a definitive answer to,' David went on to say, 'and that is, with Mary and I becoming the Terrestrial Twins, are we somehow connected with extraterrestrials? Every time I have raised the topic with Merlin he's just simply fobbed it off. When Mary and I try to discuss it we end up with a nasty headache. And I think I'll get another if I go on about it now.'

'I just think you might, Bruv,' Mary said, 'so I think that's enough about aliens for now. Perhaps we can discuss them at another time. But for now I think we should give it a rest and get back to our fishing or Mum and Dad might think something is wrong.'

'Good idea, Sis,' David said, so they did. And it helped to round off what had again been another very eventful day as they all caught some quality *double figure* carp. But the day's events and conversations also left them wondering what tomorrow might bring…

Chapter Fifteen

'THEY CAN FLY AS WELL'

They had all agreed the night before, on the way back from fishing, that Bill's suggestion to go for a session of trail horseback riding after lunch was a great idea. Everyone enjoyed riding, but had never actually done any whilst they had been on holiday.

Both David and Mary had done a lot of horse riding, as it was something their parents particularly enjoyed. They found it extremely relaxing and it was so different from the physical martial arts teaching work they were so involved in at their Martial Arts Studio.

Seemingly, Arthur and Gwen hadn't done a lot of riding, but as they always enjoyed it, they also thought the idea of trail riding sounded a really good idea.

The plan for the afternoon was to go riding after lunch following a visit to Moatcaster in the morning. But a slight change in the start time of their morning plan had allowed them to firstly call into Lawnthorpe to have a look at the entries in their Village Scarecrow Competition. A number of villages in the region held such competitions, Lawnthorpe being one of them. As it wasn't too far off their route to Moatcaster so it made sense that they call there first.

'We've heard about scarecrow competitions,' Gwen said, 'but we've never visited a village to see any of the entries.'

'It sounds a lot of fun,' Arthur said, 'or it was for those who took time out to make them. I wonder what kind we would make if we were to produce one?'

'Drossmire springs to mind,' David said. 'I think he would be able to frighten anything, let alone a few crows or other birds.'

'You're probably right there, Son,' Bill said, 'we've only seen him once, and that was more than enough for me.'

'Me too,' Sylvia said. 'He was grotesque.'

'I thought you didn't fancy him?' Mary joked.

'It wasn't a funny experience, Mary,' Sylvia replied. 'He was slimy and smelly and made my skin creep. He's an awful lot like his father, King Offalmire. It makes me feel sick just to think about that monster and our awesome involvements with him two years ago.'

'Sorry, Mum,' Mary said. 'No, he's not a joking matter. I know I will never forget my disgusting experience either. Words can't describe what I felt being held so close to his smelly body when that obnoxious Offalmire managed to grab me,' and she shuddered just thinking about it.

As they entered Lawnthorpe village, they came upon the figure of a man standing at the side of the road dressed in a one piece, dark blue overall and wearing a worker's orange safety helmet. The figure was pointing into the village.

'That's a good one,' Sylvia said. 'It looks real.'

'So do those two school children with that dog,' Mary said. 'Somebody has spent a lot of time preparing them.'

'I think this one looks like a spaceman,' Arthur said, 'and it's pretty good too.'

'There are two more here,' David said, 'they look like farm workers cutting grass with scythes.'

But as they drew nearer to them and started to slow down for a closer look, the two figures astounded everyone by leaping onto the bonnet of their car and looking like they were ready for a fight.

'Hold tight,' Bill yelled as he braked hard, catapulting their assailants on to the road in front of them.

The sudden stop hadn't bothered anyone in the car as they were all properly wearing their seat belts, which David and Mary quickly unfastened before leaping out. David moved to the left, Mary to the right.

Once out of the car they both had to use all of their athletic skills to nimbly avoid the scythes. The scythe David's attacker was swinging was a long handled and long bladed ancient type. Mary's attacker wielded a short, scimitar-type blade with which it kept aggressively attempting to slash her.

After a number of necessary cartwheels and other gymnastic manoeuvres by the twins to escape the flashing and slashing blades, the twins then cleverly took the fight to the side of the road which was a suitable place for them to be able to zap their assailants, which they did. The entities then smouldered down to the usual pool of sloppy, muddy mucus.

'Well done!' Sylvia said. 'I must say, I never expected an attack here in this peaceful village. But then I suppose we have to expect an attack anywhere.'

'And at any time,' Bill said. 'Did you not sense their presence, kids?'

'I didn't,' David said. 'Did you, Sis?'

'No, oddly enough I didn't. Not a thing. I think Drossmire has found a way of shielding his entities from us.'

'That serves to increase the danger!' David said. 'It was bad enough before when we could usually feel when they were close by. But now not being able to do so gives us an added problem, and them a possible advantage.'

'We'll all have to be really extra careful now then,' Sylvia said, 'especially if you're right and we have lost the advantage. I don't like the sound of that one bit.'

'I think we should forget the rest of the scarecrows for today and drive straight into Moatcaster,' Bill said. 'I could do with some more fishing hooks. I can get some from the tackle shop while we're there.'

'That fight you and Mary got into back there with those scarecrows was a bit of a shock,' Gwen said. 'I don't think we could have beaten them, and we certainly couldn't have zapped them to finish them off like you and Mary did.'

'You would have been able to if you rather than Mary and I had become the Terrestrial Twins,' David said. 'It's only the additional strengths and supernatural powers we have been blessed with that gives us our exceptional superhuman abilities and enable us to do what we do.'

'I've never thought of us as being exceptional or superhuman,' Mary said, 'but I suppose we are.'

'You certainly are,' Sylvia said, 'you most certainly are. And if you hadn't been blessed, none of us would be here today talking about it.'

'All right, love,' Bill said, 'we all know our twins are very special, exceptional even. But let's try to live as normal a life as we can. I know it's not easy and Drossmire's mob aren't helping. However, let's try and focus on our holiday for at least a couple of days and have some fun if and when we can. The serious stuff will no doubt keep cropping up from time to time. But unless or until it does, let's just try to be holiday-makers, tourists if you like.'

'I've never thought of us as being tourists either, Dad,' David said, 'but I suppose we are really. Well, sort of.'

Bill found a place to park in the car park just off the main road and they set off together to have a look around the town and do a bit of shopping.

As Bill wanted some more fishing hooks, he and Sylvia popped into the tackle shop near the river while both sets of twins slowly walked ahead over the bridge into the town. David walked with Gwen and Mary with Arthur.

They were almost halfway across the bridge when two quad bikes roared up behind them. Both bikes carried a driver and a passenger, all dressed in the same one-piece brown overalls they'd seen before. The four teenagers jumped up on to the parapet of the bridge to avoid being run down. Having avoided being flattened, both sets of twins leapt on to the quads and an unarmed battle commenced on each vehicle.

Although they knew full well that their lives were at stake, the teenagers nevertheless seemed to enjoy showing off their fighting skills and strengths and the whole scene moved like an orchestrated dance. The kicking, thumping, parrying, weaving and bobbing of the fighting moved down from the quads as they jumped back on to the road. It then returned up on to the quads and finally on to the parapet of the bridge. Eventually, in a last desperate effort to get away from the fight they had started, now painfully aware that they were literally being beaten, the entities leapt on to their quads and disappeared, but only after luckily succeeding in managing to unbalance and push both sets of twins off the parapet of the bridge in the direction of the river below.

Bill and Sylvia had just emerged from the tackle shop to see both sets of twins disappear from sight over the edge of the bridge just as the quad bikes and their drivers and passengers disappeared into thin air.

But the shock and horror on their parents' faces quickly changed to surprise, as David and Mary appeared each cradling their partner in their arms, and gently glided up and back over the parapet to put them down on the footpath, close to Bill and Sylvia who were relieved to see all four of them.

'Thank God you're all right,' Sylvia said as she gripped the arms of her twins. 'When I saw all of you go over, I expected you to be in the river.'

'No, thankfully not,' Gwen said. 'And, what do you know? We've discovered David and Mary can fly too!'

'We were amazed,' Arthur said. 'The entities somehow managed to push the four of us over the edge and we began to fall. Then, amazingly, David and Mary managed to catch us and lifted us up and back here. You arrived in time to see us coming back up and over the parapet. It was fantastic.'

'Brillfanmagical is the word,' David said, 'try to remember it, Arthur. Brillfanmagical!' And they all enjoyed a good laugh as they brushed down and straightened their clothes.

They were just about to move on, when they noticed two couples standing frozen on the town side of the bridge and looking at them in complete amazement.

'They must be white witches or from a white witch's family,' David said, 'and they witnessed what happened.'

'Poor things,' Mary said. 'We'll have to clear their minds. We can't leave them standing there like that.'

'You had better do it quickly,' Sylvia said, 'before somebody notices, or it could develop into a tricky situation.'

They all agreed. David and Mary then stood behind both couples and, in voices directed straight at the back of their heads, spoke to them and sent telepathic messages at the same time saying, 'You saw nothing unusual here this morning, continue walking to where you were going and forget everything you witnessed.'

Both couples blinked their eyes and started walking over the bridge in the direction of the car park. One of the men looked puzzled. He glanced over the parapet, shook his head and shrugged his shoulders then rejoined his partner.

'That was some fight,' Arthur said. 'I don't think I have ever been tested to such a degree.'

'That's because no one in the past has been seriously trying to kill you,' Mary said, 'and I'm glad they didn't succeed.' She reached out and gripped his hand.

'Thanks for catching me, David,' Gwen said. 'Is there no end to your talents?' She took hold of his hand. David just grinned one of his cheeky grins as they all walked into town as three couples, all happily holding hands.

The shopping trip was a success for everybody. All the girls found new tops, and the lads bought new shorts. And as Bill had bought some hooks and a couple of floats, they all thought it had been a good morning, apart from the two incidents, which were fully discussed over lunch.

David also answered Arthur's question as to how, when and why Red, their friendly dragon, had moved into the King's Banqueting Hall in Moatcaster Castle. He explained how Red had been in a waterlogged tomb below a hill with a white dragon, which he mythologically and repeatedly had to fight and beat, sometimes on a daily basis.

Because of this, he got Merlin to produce a replica of him to occasionally fight the white dragon. This then allowed him to move into the King's Banqueting Hall to keep an eye on things for Merlin. Red took his role of being the guardian of the hidden Crystal Tower's contents very seriously, and only occasionally popped back to see Snowy, the name he gave to the white dragon he was very good friends with really. But he only occasionally visited Snowy when Merlin was free to sit-in for him, as there was no way he would ever leave his guard post. The Crystal Tower was too important to be left unguarded.

The fights that were staged between Red and Snowy were just for show really and to support the mythological stories. As Red had liked being named Red by the twins, he was very pleased his white dragon friend was happy when he named him Snowy.

Having enjoyed their lunches, everyone said how much they were looking forward to the trail horseback riding that Bill had suggested for the afternoon. It was such a warm day and even though it had been a great shopping trip it had been a bit tiring. So the idea of enjoying a steady ride in the attractive Castershire countryside, relaxing on the back of a horse, seemed a perfect way of spending the rest of the afternoon.....What could possibly go wrong?

Chapter Sixteen

SUSPENDED ANIMATION

'I'm told the riding session we're going on lasts for about two hours and takes in bridleways, woodland, lanes and walks by the river,' Bill said, as they pulled up in the riding centre parking area. 'I've been looking forward to doing this for years and as it's such a lovely afternoon, I think we should all enjoy it.'

'I don't think we've done as much riding as your family,' Arthur said, 'but Gwen and I are really looking forward to it like you are, Mister Knight. It's bound to be fun when we're in such good company.'

'Here, here!' Gwen said, 'Arthur's right. The company's the best and as it's a lovely warm afternoon, it should be great. Just don't expect us to race anybody though.'

'We'll not do that,' David said, 'but I expect there will be a bit of trotting. And I promise I will catch you if you fall off,' he joked.

'Nobody's going to fall off,' Bill said. 'I doubt very much if we'll be made to go very fast anywhere.'

Having paid their dues and received an introductory chat of does and don'ts and sorted out their head gear, they set off for a couple of hours of fun.

It was a great experience, especially as the saddles were of the type cowboys in the Wild West used, which were very comfortable. All of which helped make the pleasant and peaceful afternoon something very different and enjoyable.

Unfortunately, just after entering a wooded area, their afternoon became a nightmare on horseback, as their horses were panicked into bolting by two riders on noisy motorbikes. The bike riders drove close to and between the horses, then in circles around them, revving their engines purposely to unnerve them. The Knight family managed to calm and bring their mounts under control, but as Arthur and Gwen were not such experienced riders they were unable to steady their horses. The inevitable then occurred. Their horses, having been so badly tormented and alarmed by the motorbikes, jumped and whirled about one more time before bolting. Now completely out of control they rushed under some of the trees by the side of the lane taking Arthur and Gwen with them, who were now tightly gripping on to their saddles for dear life.

What happened next was terrifying....... Just as Gwen and Arthur's horses reached a point where some of the tree branches protruded over the lane, two noosed ropes dropped on to them. The first dropped around Arthur's shoulders and tightened, immediately lifting and yanking him off his horse to hang helplessly suspended above the track.

Sylvia and Mary then shrieked in panic and Bill and David shouted Gwen's name, as the noose of the second rope, which had dropped around Gwen began to slide up from her chest as she struggled and tightened round her neck like a hangman's noose before tugging her off her horse. Having been dragged from her saddle, she was now left suspended, swinging on the rope which was now tightly knotted round her neck.

David literally flew from his horse to grab, lift and support her, enabling Mary who had joined him to gently loosen and remove the noose from her neck. At the same time Bill lifted Arthur while Sylvia loosened the rope around his chest. The motorbikes were no longer anywhere to be seen.

Having lovingly taken Gwen in his arms, David gently lowered her on to the soft grass at the side of the lane, and asked Mary to quickly go over to the young teenage Trail Guide from the Riding Centre who had been accompanying them and freeze her mind until they could sort things out. The poor girl had been awestruck by everything she had just so unbelievingly witnessed.

Sylvia dropped to her knees at the side of her son and couldn't help crying as she looked at him, taking his hand and asked him the question that had to be on everyone's lips.

'Is... Is she...?'

'No, Mum, she isn't... She isn't dead.'

'Oh, thank the gods for that.'

'She hasn't really got a pulse though,' David continued. 'I think she must be in some sort of suspended animation. But no, thankfully she's not dead.'

'What are we going to do?' Arthur asked, having now joined everyone kneeling round Gwen's still and seemingly lifeless body. Tears welled in his eyes as he looked at the motionless body of his twin sister.

'I think we can answer that question for you, Arthur,' said a voice above him. And there, now sitting on a branch above their heads were the seven friendly guardian magpies. 'The Gods of the Terrestrial Light have asked us to help and told us what to do,' the spokesman bird said.

'It might sound a little strange, but trust me, it will be all right. And more to the point, Arthur, it will work.'

'Anything you can do to help Gwen is fine by me, magpie. We have always trusted you in the past, so there is no reason for us to doubt you now. Thank you!' said David.

'As I said,' the magpie continued, 'it may seem a little odd, but you must all act quickly.' None of them needed telling twice. 'You all have to get back on your horses. You will first need to get the Trail Guide back onto hers. She'll be all right in the state Mary has put her in.'

'We will hold and support Gwen in place on her horse when you've lifted her on. Then you must all return to your own horses. We have no time to waste.'

Everyone was astounded by the magpie's unusual instructions, but they did what they were told as quickly as they could.

With the magpies' help they collected the horses together then David and Mary gently lifted and lowered Gwen back onto her horse, her head drooping sickeningly forward on to her chest. The magpies then took over to hold her in place including raising her head.

'Right, David,' the magpie said, 'you and Mary must now hold hands in the twinning position.'

They did as they were told.

'Okay. Now, link together telepathically and ask the Gods to move you into a parallel time dimension that will allow all of you to be taken back in time. You will subsequently be returned from this dimension to the time when you first arrived at the riding stables.'

'What a great idea,' both David and Mary said together. Then, tightly gripping hands they mentally said in unison, 'Please, Gods of the Terrestrial Light, take us all back about three quarters of an hour through a parallel time dimension to return and emerge at the time when we first arrived at the stables this afternoon.'

The instant they thought it, they all vanished. There wasn't a sound or a flash of light, they simply disappeared. They were all amazed and so very grateful when only microseconds later, they found themselves loosening themselves from their car seat belts, having just arrived at the centre for their afternoon of being in the saddle.

As they stepped out of the car, Gwen was surprised to see everyone look up and heard them say, 'Thank you. Thank you very much!'

'Did I miss something?' she asked, looking a little puzzled.

'No, love,' David said, as he took her hand. 'But from now on, I'll always think of you as a swinging chick!' He didn't expect a laugh from anyone for that remark, so wasn't disappointed when he didn't get one.

'It's an in joke, love,' he said. 'I'll tell you about it another time.'

Would you believe it, they all had a most enjoyable afternoon. They knew the countryside was attractive but being able to better absorb it from their high-seated position on the back of a tall horse just steadily plodding along, made it something special. It also gave five of the six of them a better memory this time than the horrible one they had so sadly experienced when they had first ridden out.

Following the afternoon's trail riding, it was agreed a trip to Scour Bay for tea would be a good idea. David became the appointed driver on this occasion.

He was pleased when they arrived at the bay to find a spot to park in the harbour car park and suggested they buy ice creams. They all opted to have a cornet and to sit on the top of the harbour wall to watch some small yachts which were racing across the mouth of the bay.

David had just passed a comment about the warning sign not to feed the seagulls, when one swooped over his shoulder and cleverly whipped the ice cream and cornet out of his hand as he was lifting it to his mouth.

135

'I thought you had quick reflexes, Bruv,' Mary joked. 'You weren't fast enough that time, were you?'

'Did you see it?' David said in a joking but shocked tone. 'It frightened the…

'That will do, Son!' Bill said 'I hope no policeman saw you though, or you might get arrested for feeding the seagulls!' His joke made everyone laugh.

Even David could see the funny side of it. 'I bet that ice cream salesman trains them to do that, hoping his customers will go back to buy another.'

As David and Mary wanted to show Arthur and Gwen the entrance to the old mine where the bats were, and tell them about the events which had occurred two years earlier at Peg Dyke Sands, during tea they decided they would take a walk along the coastal path.

So after tea they set off on their coastal path walk. When they reached it they fooled about in the tunnel the path went through, making supposed ghost noises and laughing just for fun. Their child-like behaviour gave them a rare opportunity to relax and just enjoy themselves. Even Bill and Sylvia joined in until some other people also entered the tunnel, which made them quiet down and behave normally. But all of them really had enjoyed the bit of harmless fun.

'This is where the bats were coming out of two years ago,' David said when they reached the sealed off former entrance to the old mine.

'You should have seen David holding a crisp bag and asking the bats to deposit some droppings in it,' Mary laughingly said. 'It really did have to be seen to be believed.'

'But they did it,' David said, 'then one turned into a huge thing and whisked me and Sis up and took us more than half a mile or so out to sea before dropping us.'

'And a couple of dolphins brought us back,' Mary said, grinning like a Cheshire cat. 'The ride was absolutely great!'

'Wow, I bet it was,' Gwen said, feeling a little envious.

It wasn't long before the footpath running parallel and close to the beach brought them to where the waters of Peg Dyke ran out of the land and weaved its way down the sand to the sea. The running water then gave David and Mary the opportunity to show Arthur and Gwen how they had raced the flat sea shells. And they all had some fun doing it again.

Apart from having to splat a huge bat that attacked them on the way back to Scour Bay, the evening was a lot of fun and enjoyed by everyone. David had the last word before they drove back to their cottage for a nightcap of drinking chocolate to end the day saying, 'Don't those things just drive you batty!'

Having arrived back at their holiday cottage, they had just got comfortably seated in the lounge, when David asked the question that had been buzzing around in his and Mary's heads for more than two years. And it seemingly wasn't a surprise to either of his parents when he said, 'We keep talking about the Thirteen Treasures of Britain that firstly King Offalmire wanted to get at, and we had to stop him. And now his son, Drossmire, appears to be after them. But I for one haven't a clue as to why, or even what, any of them are. So come on Dad, what are they and why are they so important?'

'And how could Drossmire misuse them?' Mary asked.

'To be honest, I'm surprised it's taken you this long before you got round to asking,' Bill replied. 'But sit back with your chocolate and I'll tell you what I know. It's not a lot, but I think it will give you the general picture and allow you to understand why the Terrestrial Light Gods are so keen to keep them from falling into the wrong hands. Currently the wrong hands belong to Drossmire, which also makes it easy for all of us to understand why Merlin took so much trouble to hide them in the first place.

'It's almost like a *Once upon a time story*. If my memory serves me right, it all started in the fifteenth and sixteenth centuries, possibly even as far back as the twelfth.

'Some say there are more than Thirteen Treasures and there are various lists as to what they are and what they might be used for. But the general opinion is that if they fall into the wrong hands, and particularly if their values and uses were then supernaturally warped or modified, the results could be catastrophic. Life on Earth as we know it could be critically altered. Or possibly worse, may even be destroyed.'

'But what are the Treasures and how could they affect us all so much?' David asked.

'I can't remember them all but I can remember some,' Bill replied, 'I'm not even sure I remember much of the detail that goes with them either, but I'll do my best and have a go.

'One of them is a special sword. It can somehow burst into flame and I believe the owner can ask for and receive whatever he or she wants. That could lead to chaos if it was misused. Another one is a horn and whatever kind of drink the owner might ask for would appear in it. Which means the owner could end up with a lot of something he could do harm with if it were magically tainted or poisoned. A hamper is another one on the list that can magically multiply the amount of food put in it a hundred times, which sounds all right, but if it were poisoned food and it was distributed how many might suffer and or die?

There is also another one to do with food and obviously the same misuse could apply. A cloak of invisibility is also on the list. If that was supernaturally made to grow, it could be used to blanket out whole towns or counties or worse, even countries.

'I'm sure it wasn't ever envisaged that the treasures might ever be misused in that way, but perhaps Offalmire or others were not around when they were being supernaturally created. If you weren't totally sure before you can now see why you two were created in your special roles as the Terrestrial Twins. The exceptional and awesome abilities with which you have been blessed were given to you to ensure the safety and security of the world as we know it. You can now see why protecting the Thirteen Treasures of Britain, which Merlin so cleverly and safely hid, has been and is of such paramount importance.

'But you two are the ones that make a difference. Terrestrial beings, whatever they are, but particularly human beings, have you two on their side looking after them. I for one am more than happy we are in your team. I would hate to think you were our opponents or enemies.'

'Thanks for all the info, Dad. I am sure we all now have a much better picture of the reason the Treasures must be protected from falling into the wrong hands,' Mary said looking at the perplexed expression on David's face. 'What's up, Bruv, cat got your tongue?'

'I was just thinking, Sis. It's a ruddy good job Mum and Dad managed to get us born in the first place, or we couldn't have done so well in any place!'

Chapter Seventeen

TROUBLE IN CLIFFTHORPE BAY

It had been agreed during the previous day's lunch that visiting Cliffthorpe Bay would be a good idea, so when Gwen and Arthur arrived at the cottage after breakfast, it was to Cliffthorpe Bay they all went.

'I love the view of the harbour,' Sylvia said as they turned down the street that gave them a magnificent view overlooking both the beach and the harbour. They were unlucky trying to find an on-street place to park, the town being such a popular place in the holiday season, so David drove to the multi-storey car park to park.

Walking into town, it was agreed they would first visit what remained of Cliffthorpe Castle, its remains were situated on the hill overlooking the bay. Then, to save walking round the bay to the museum, which was to be the second location on their impromptu tour, they decided to take a short-cut and walk across the sands. They also had intended calling in to explore the old fort known by the locals as 'the bunion'.

Bill had somehow managed with a couple of phone calls to acquire permission to visit the fort, as it was not normally open to the public. With an expected low tide it was going to be possible to reach both the museum and the old fort, 'the bunion', by walking across the beach, as both were on the rocky peninsula on the far side of the bay. A representative of the owners who Bill had spoken to, had suggested they enjoy the walk across the sand and meet him there to enable him to let them in and show them round at eleven o'clock. So they had all agreed that Cliffthorpe Castle would be the place to visit first.

Both David and Mary had great fun when they arrived at the pair of cannons situated at the base of the castle and facing out towards 'the bunion', informing Arthur and Gwen how they had been shot at by a similar cannon two years earlier when they were on Fishington harbour. They then went on to explain how the invisible missile had ripped through the crab pots close to where they were standing, and how they had needed to run for their lives.

'It was one of those events that you just can't clear from your mind,' Mary said in a rather serious voice. David nodded in agreement.

However, shortly after their arrival at Cliffthorpe Castle they all received a bit of a shock. It happened as they were ascending a flight of steps in the castle grounds. Sylvia had spotted a small common lizard close to the side of the steps. Apparently it was one of the places where they can be found in Castershire. She was about to point it out to the others when she gave out a yell as it suddenly and amazingly quickly grew to the size of a medium-sized alligator and frighteningly charged at her. It was only her speedy reactions and an acrobatic cartwheel that saved her from being bitten.

Having firstly snapped at Sylvia, it then had a go at Arthur and also at Gwen. Sadly for the alligator, both of them were quicker, and just as Sylvia had done, they both nimbly jumped away from its evil looking, gnashing jaws full of sharp, pointed teeth. It then had a go at Bill who had moved closer to assist his wife if she needed it, but again it fortunately failed in its attempt to grab his leg, as he too was far too quick for it.

'I think we can all do without this kind of interference this morning,' David calmly said. But before he could do what he was about to do, another huge similar creature, which had suddenly materialized behind him, grabbed hold of his right ankle giving him a nasty nip. His reflexes kicked in as he shook it off and zapped it just as Mary did the same to the first one. Both creatures then turned into the usual pools of green and brown, muddy mucus.

'That's going to leave a nasty bruise on your foot, love,' Sylvia said, wincing as she said it. David just shrugged his shoulders.

'I had no warning they were here, Sis, did you?'

'No, Bruv, nothing!' Mary replied. 'I sensed no danger at all. It's very obvious Drossmire is still somehow managing to mask-out any warning of the presence of any Other World entities, and I don't like it one bit.'

'We have to remember that retribution is the only thought in Drossmire's evil mind,' Bill said, 'and he's not going to rest until he has succeeded, or so he thinks.'

'Tomorrow is the big day at Tinker's Hall,' David said, 'that's when Drossmire gets his comeuppance. We can develop a plan of action later, but I must confess I am really looking forward to some sort of medieval-type fighting or jousting. The idea really appeals to me.'

'Me too,' Mary added. 'I feel sure it's something we will all be able to enjoy. We are all accomplished fighters, so it should be great and could even be, as Merlin said, *fun!*'

'But let's not forget Drossmire is an evil and devious character,' Bill said, 'we have no idea what he might get up to, so we will have to be on our guard all the time we are there or we might come unstuck, and that could prove fatal. Six of us will be walking into Tinker's Hall, let's just make sure six of us walk out.'

Sylvia broke into Bill's conversation at this point to inform everyone that the tide was now well out and that they ought to be making for 'the bunion' for their appointment to be shown around the fort.

'I'm sure you can tell us something about that place, Dad?' Mary said. 'Can't you?'

'Not a lot, love. All I can remember about the building,' Bill said as they walked through the now virtually dry harbour and on to the beach, 'is that the hundred yards or so of rocky land that juts out into the sea, which we can now see on the far side of the bay, was first used as a site for a fortress something like a thousand years ago. A number of similar defences have been erected there over the years including the present fort which was erected at the onset of World War One. That was about the same time the lifeboat station was built in which the museum is now housed. It's easy to see why the locals nicknamed the fort "the bunion" though, as it stands out on the end of the peninsula like a bunion on somebody's toe.

'The remains of the fort were used at sometime in the eighties and nineties as a mushroom growing complex but I don't think it has been used for many years.'

'I told you he would know a bit,' Mary joked.

As they neared the outcrop of rock on which the fort was situated, the entrance to a huge cave came into view.

'Wow!' Arthur said. 'I had no idea this was here.'

'Me neither,' said Mary. 'I don't think any of us apart from Mum and Dad did.'

'It's huge,' Gwen said.

'It's a heck of a cave,' Arthur said.

And as they slowly walked in, they all found themselves looking up and around what turned out to be a huge cavern with smaller caves off to the side. The outcrop of rock which formed the peninsula was a massive section of limestone protruding literally out of the sand and adjoining and forming part of the cliffs of the bay which otherwise were mainly volcanic rock. Much of the lower part of the limestone headland below the fort contained not only this huge cavern, but was also riddled with a complex of smaller caves. All of the caves had been formed from cracks in the rock which had been worn away for centuries by the eroding action of the sea and weather.

'What's the word, Son?' Bill asked of David.

'Magnormous, Dad,' was David's reply, 'magnormous!'

'It's huge as well,' Mary joked.

Sadly, what none of them had noticed as they stood gazing up and around, was something wriggling just below the surface of the sand and moving towards Bill. They only realized what was happening, which made them all jump with shock, when Bill's surprised and painful yell echoed around the cavern.

A huge lugworm, for that was what it was, looking a bit like an elongated loo brush, had grabbed his left ankle. As the majority of the evil creature's body was firmly anchored under the sand, Bill had no chance of pulling away from the nasty worm that now so tightly gripped him.

It was at that moment that all hell seemed to be let loose, as following a huge explosive sound somewhere close to the castle, a sort of invisible projectile came screaming through the air and tore into the cave rebounding from wall to wall, ripping out large boulders and dozens of smaller chunks of rock, which flew everywhere.

The mayhem was caused by a cannon ball, which having materialized finally fell and rolled close to Sylvia's feet, making her instinctively jump towards the cave entrance.

'Follow your Mum's example,' Bill yelled, and get out of this hell hole as quickly as you can before we are all ripped to shreds by the damned things being shot into here. It's obvious Drossmire has set-up another trap, and has also managed to use one of the castle's damned cannons. He really means to kill us all, or as many of us as he can. I'm sure he's also using these ruddy lugworms to hold us in place 'till we're hit by missiles or shrapnel.' Bill could see two more very big lugworms tunnelling through the sand from holes in the cavern wall towards them.

'The missiles will ricochet round the cavern and rip us all to pieces if we don't get out. We all need to move and get out! So go! Out! Get out now!'

Another missile came screaming in as he spoke and terrifyingly rebounded around the cavern from wall to wall sending fragments of rock flying dangerously everywhere. Pulling with all their might the rest of the group desperately tried to free Bill. Then David, having knelt down, put his finger close to the offending worm's head and zapped it. It immediately let go. He and Mary then zapped the remaining worms just as they surfaced, at the same time managing to avoid more of the rebounding missiles and shrapnel that flew recklessly around the cavern.

Fortunately they all managed to get out safely although they were badly shaken and shocked by what had happened. Thankfully, apart from just a few slight scratches, none of them were seriously hurt.

'I don't think we'll bother phoning that guy later to apologize for not showing up to be shown around the old fort,' Bill said, 'I feel sure it was a very clever and devious put up job just to try and get us killed. Yet again we've been cleverly duped. And there's no way we're going to hang around out here on the sands any longer either. We're like sitting ducks.' They all agreed and sensibly sprinted out of the cannon's range and only slowed down when they reached the relative safety of the harbour.

'It's a good job what happened occurred in a slightly different parallel time,' Sylvia said as they continued on towards the town, 'or everyone in the bay would have heard the noise. It would have been terrifying.'

'I think we were all a bit scared, Mum, never mind all those who couldn't hear it,' Mary said. 'I have decided I really don't like cannons or giant lugworms either.'

'Me neither,' added Gwen. 'I don't ever want to experience anything like that again.'

'I certainly never expected us to ever again be shot at by a cannon like we were two years ago in Fishington harbour!' Sylvia added. 'I think we just experienced the worst case of déjà vu and I don't ever want it to happen again.'

'Do you think it's possible that Drossmire really could have somehow arranged for us to visit the fort, to lure us into that cave, Dad?' David asked, in a slightly bewildered tone.

'I hadn't given it a thought, Son, until we had problems in the cave, but yes, I think he did. He knew that a cannon was available and that our curiosity would take us into the cavern. What we all have just been subjected to ought to tell us just how cleverly devious he is. We must never underestimate him, ever.'

As lunch seemed to be next on the agenda, they opted for a café overlooking the end of the harbour and beach, but they all had difficulty clearing their minds. What might the afternoon have in store for them?

Chapter Eighteen

FUN THAT WENT WRONG

During lunch, Bill asked Arthur and Gwen a few questions about their parents, as up to now they only knew their surname was Dey.

'Dad's name is Gareth, Mum's is Megan,' Arthur replied, 'and if I remember correctly, Dad was born in a little hamlet just outside of Fishington. I can't remember the name of the place and we haven't been to see his old house yet, but he says we might do sometime.'

'Yes, that's right,' said Gwen, 'and Mum was born in a cottage on the other side of the town. They met at a white witches meeting which had been called to discuss the fact that King Offalmire was growing larger and stronger. He was bragging that after he discovered its location, he would one day be capable of breaking through the barrier that Merlin had placed around the hidden Crystal Tower holding the Thirteen Treasures of Britain, and happily misuse them. But both Mum and Dad stopped practising the white witch's arts just after we were born.'

'Mister Knight and I attended similar meetings for the same reasons,' Sylvia said.

'What does your dad do?' Mary asked.

'Now that's an interesting question,' replied Arthur, 'and to be honest, we don't really know.' His reply brought puzzled expressions to all the Knight family faces.

Gwen then took up the story. 'He and Mum own an outdoor activities and boy's toys warehouse on the outskirts of Pullister that Mum runs with our help plus a couple of other staff. Dad is often away doing his thing.' This brought more puzzled expressions, but Gwen continued to explain. 'Dad was for many years in some sort of special elite force. We don't know which one as he said much about it.

'When he left he became a freelance special agent and criminologist and his investigative skills and services are regularly used by the police and various government departments. We're not really sure, but we think for at least the last year or so he has been working just for one special department, but we don't know any more than that.'

'What a brillfanmagical job,' David said, 'I think I could enjoy doing something like that.'

'Couldn't we all,' Mary said, 'it sounds fascinating.'

'Joking apart,' Bill said, 'as you two grow older and as your exceptional supernatural powers grow with you, your powers of deduction and reasoning will also grow. If you think about it, linking them with your physical abilities, you could very well become really competent sleuths, as I am sure Gareth is. A job like that would be right up your street.'

'Does he travel the world much then?' Sylvia asked.

'He sometimes does,' Gwen replied, 'but a lot of the work he does is based here in the UK.'

'Is he able to spend much time with you?' Sylvia asked.

'Quite a bit really,' replied Arthur. 'I would say he's with us almost half of the year and we do all sorts of outdoor pursuits. Recently we were all enjoying some scrambling, when a little blonde haired girl suddenly appeared in front of Dad's motorbike and he ended up breaking both legs in the accident that resulted when he tried to avoid her. The little girl then just disappeared. It was obviously a supernatural event and it prevented him being able to come to Castershire with us.'

'It was probably engineered by Drossmire to keep your dad's brain at home in an attempt to reduce the effectiveness of our collective abilities,' Bill said.

'You are probably right, Mister Knight,' Arthur replied, 'that's what we thought when we learned from Merlin that our assistance might be needed. Drossmire obviously thought that all the family would be able to come and possibly be able to help, in whatever capacity it may, but as you know, Mum rightly stayed at home to look after Dad following his accident.'

'But you have both been able to help,' Mary said. 'You helped Mum and Merlin as well as yourselves escape from Tollvale Castle, and you certainly helped in the fighting on the quad bikes in Moatcaster, and we've all got to know each other and I think it's just great.'

'Me too, Sis,' David added, 'but talking about quads, I saw an advert referring to a quad bike centre not far from here, so I suggest we go and have a session. It should be fun.'

Everyone agreed it was a great idea and, having managed to return to their car just before their parking ticket ran out, they headed out of Cliffthorpe Bay looking forward to enjoying some four-wheeled fun.

They were all bitterly disappointed when they arrived at the centre to learn that because of its popularity they needed to pre-book and there were no openings that afternoon. As they were at the centre, David asked if they could look around and examine some of the machines, and everyone described them as great, cool or awesome.

They all agreed that it would also make a lot of sense that while they were there they should book a session for another day. They had just started to give their details to a young woman booking them in when the phone rang in the office behind her, and she politely apologized before leaving to answer it. Her telephone conversation lasted only a couple of minutes and they were all delighted when she returned and told them that the caller had been the organizer of the group who had booked the next session phoning to cancel. And if they still wanted to have the session now, they could.

'Yes please,' Bill said, 'we'll be delighted to have it, but it will only be for four. I'm sorry to say I haven't got around to being able to print my own money yet and the holiday is far from over! The kids will enjoy it more if they are on their own anyway, so it will just be the four of them. My wife and I will sit this one out.'

Both David and Mary knew it would be a pointless exercise trying to change their dad's mind, even though Arthur and Gwen were quite happy to pay for themselves. So David gratefully accepted his dad's generosity on behalf of the four of them. They then went off to receive their instructions and about the do's and don'ts of quad trial riding at the centre. Then to the changing rooms to be kitted-out with the necessary protective and safety gear which the centre supplied.

Shortly after the four of them had waved their goodbyes and roared away, Sylvia quite casually asked the assistant who was walking past them and who had received the phone call if she knew the reason for the next group cancelling their session.

'Yes, they did tell me and were a bit upset too.'

'Because of having to cancel?' Sylvia asked. She and Bill were then amazed at the assistant's reply.

'No, it was because of what happened to two of their group. They were on the beach at Cliffthorpe Bay this morning when two of the men went into the big cave under 'the bunion' because they'd been caught short. But they didn't come out, so their wives went in to look for them.'

With apprehension in her voice Sylvia then asked what had happened to them.

'They don't know. Both men were laid on the sand in the cave. Both of them were unconscious and bleeding from head and shoulder wounds, and one had lost a little finger, plus they both had bite marks on their ankles. The woman who rang was at the hospital and was told that they are both suffering from concussion, but are in no real danger. They were also told they would be kept in overnight for observation. It seems they were part of a white witch's get-together taking place in Cliffthorpe Bay.'

Sylvia thanked her for her information and as the young woman walked away Sylvia turned to Bill, the colour visually draining from her cheeks...

Out on the quad trail both sets of twins were really enjoying themselves. The machines were first class semi-automatic and powerful quad bikes and responded to everything they asked of them. The four of them were really enjoying riding and racing them through and over all the various types of terrain, sometimes climbing then descending at speed and whizzing round corners. It was great fun.

There were many man-made as well as natural obstacles including trees to negotiate, all of which tested their abilities and added to the fun. The flat field areas gave the opportunity to speed, whilst the cambered sections were hairy, sometimes almost impossible to cope with, and the water problems needed extra thought.

It was all great fun until, as Arthur was attempting to cope with a corner amongst the trees, a young girl suddenly appeared right in his path and he had no option but to try to avoid her. In his attempt to miss her, he was forced to steer off the trail and sadly hit a rock in the grass which shot his quad into an involuntary roll and he cracked his head on a tree as his bike went over. On the track the little girl vanished as quickly as she had appeared, a sickly satisfied smile on her face.

David and Mary sensed Arthur's difficulty at the same time and roared back to where he was. Mary arrived just after her brother and looked on as he knelt down to check Arthur's pulse. 'He's alright, Sis, he's still with us.'

'Thank the Gods for that,' Mary sighed as she also knelt down beside her brother and Arthur.

Both Mary and her mum had achieved their first aid certificates, just in case they ever needed them and to comply with the health and safety regulations at their martial arts studio, so she knew exactly what to do. Having checked Arthur all over carefully but thoroughly, she announced to David that he could be moved.

'I'll fly him over to the side of their buildings, Sis,' David said. 'I noticed they had an accident room so it makes sense we take him in there to examine him properly. We can carry him in after I get him there.'

Then, with Mary's help, he carefully lifted and gathered Arthur in his arms and after amazingly becoming invisible, re-emerged to normality at the side of the buildings. Mary had also made herself invisible and re-appeared alongside of him.

'That's another first, Bruv,' she said. 'I didn't know we could make ourselves invisible.'

'Me neither,' grinned David, 'it was brill. It just felt like the right thing to do at the time.'

Mary went into the building first to alert the female assistant as to what had happened, not knowing at this time about the little girl, only that Arthur had been involved in an accident.

The young woman led them all into the accident room and asked David to lay him on the stretcher bed. She told them that she was the centre's First Aider and that she would examine him to ascertain whether or not he needed to be seen by a doctor. She then asked them to leave the room, which they did.

Outside, they met their mum and dad with Gwen, who had come across Arthur's upturned quad and the two abandoned ones, and had returned to the office to see what was happening.

'He's all right, Gwen,' Mary said taking hold of her hands to comfort her. 'The centre's First Aider is checking him over. I did it before David flew him back and there are no bones broken, but he certainly had a crack on the head.'

Sylvia told them how they had managed to get in this afternoon and why there had been a cancellation, and that the two young men, white witches, had been injured in the cave.

'That's unbelievable,' David said, 'but they would have been perfectly all right if it wasn't for being white witches. If they had just been holidaymakers nothing would have happened to them......Hang on a minute though, what if all of this has been contrived to get us here. Have we again been duped? Arthur! He could be in trouble. That First Aider isn't one or she would have phoned for an ambulance straight away!'

Then, quick as a flash, he charged into the accident room with Mary close on his heels. Fortunately they were just in time to save Arthur as the supposed First Aider was about to bite his neck with two fangs that were now clearly protruding from the sides of her mouth, set into what was now a rather ugly face.

David flung himself bodily at the entity, for it was now obvious what she was, but she just hissed like a cat and vanished and David found himself grasping at thin air, that wasn't very fresh following her parting disgusting fart.

'Is Arthur all right?' Mary and Gwen asked together.

'Yes, he appears to be,' David replied. Then turning to Mary said, 'Can't we bathe his head with cold water and give him a drink or something.'

'No need to, David, I'm all right,' said the voice from the stretcher bed as Arthur slowly sat up and steadily swung his legs over the edge. Mary couldn't contain herself and flung her arms round his neck. Gwen had to settle for holding his hand.

'Steady, love, watch my bruise.' And he really did have a whopper above his right eye where his protective helmet had been knocked into his forehead. It looked very sore. 'And before you ask me what happened, I had the same type of experience that Dad had. I had to brake hard to avoid a little girl, who I then saw grin and disappear just before I passed out. Fortunately I only cracked my head, but it was a good job I was wearing a helmet.' He carefully touched the steadily rising reddened bump.

'It was your neck they wanted to get at, not break your legs or anything else, Arthur,' David said having informed everyone of what he saw when he burst into the room seconds earlier. 'They only needed you to be unconscious to enable that evil bitch to get her teeth into you, literally.'

'You don't mean she was a….a vampire, David, do you?' Sylvia asked in a trembling voice.

'Sorry to disappoint you, Mum, but yes, she most certainly was…. a vampire.'

Before they could say anything else they were interrupted by a middle-aged man wearing grease stained overalls and with oily smudges on his cheek who was obviously very surprised to see them gathered together in the room.

'What the hell are you lot doing in my store room?'

And sure enough, there was now a sign on the open door that clearly said "Store Room" not "First Aid Room".

'There shouldn't be any members of the public here at all this afternoon. The centre's closed today and tomorrow to do bike servicing and I've come in here for some gaskets. You had better clear off before the boss sees you and reports you to the police for burglary or trespass or something.'

With that he reached over to remove two gaskets that were now hanging on the wall. It really was a store room.

The stretcher bed had changed its appearance and was very obviously a workshop bench with a small vice fixed to one end, close to where Arthur's head had been lying only minutes before, and there were shelves on the walls full of all sorts of mechanical bits, tins, bottles and boxes.

The six so called trespassers headed for their car as fast as their legs would take them, all hoping some sort of normality would quickly come back into their lives.

'Let's just get the hell out of here, and quickly, Bill,' Sylvia said as she hastily clicked her seat belt in place, 'we can talk about this mad afternoon later.'

And Bill didn't need telling twice...

Chapter Nineteen

A HUGE SHADOW APPEARED

They chose to leave the Cliffthorpe Bay area by travelling towards Crossthorpe. As Tinker's Hall was on the edge of the village, they would be able to have a closer look at it and the surrounding area to give them a better idea about the layout of the place. Tinker's Hall being the location they now considered to probably be the venue for the main event the following day. So it made a lot of sense that they learned as much about it as they could.

There was very little traffic on what turned out to be a very pleasant route and the heat of the day and the bright sunlight and variety of roadside flowers had brought out a whole host of different kinds of butterflies. Everyone was beginning to feeling a little more relaxed, especially after their dreadful quad bike and vampire experiences.

But just when everything seemed to be so much better and going so well, and a couple of them were almost on the point of sleeping, Bill was suddenly forced to violently brake, which tested everybody's seat belts. A large feathered creature looking something like an overgrown ostrich had run across the road in front of their car, having jumped the hedge between the trees to the right of them. In fact, if it had been any closer it would have run into them.

'What the hell was that?' Sylvia questioned, almost choking with surprise and shock as she said it.

'I think it was a prehistoric bird, Mum,' Mary said, as though she didn't believe what she was saying. 'It must have been supernaturally turned into a proper creature as there are lots of prehistoric animal models in an ancient creatures visiting centre close to where we are. Let's hope there aren't going to be anymore, even if they are in a slightly different parallel time slot, or they should be.'

'What with the creatures at Cliffthorpe Castle and what happened in the cavern on the beach followed by the unforgettable quad bike event,' Sylvia said, 'and now this thing. I for one can do without any more nerve racking experiences today, thank you very much!'

'We hear you, Mum,' David said, 'but apart from that prehistoric park, there's also a wildlife and leisure park near here as well. There are all sorts of live animals in there, perhaps it's after one of them for a meal. It possibly doesn't realize it isn't real.'

Just as he finished speaking, the sun was suddenly blocked out by the huge shape of an enormous prehistoric creature towering over them. It had arrived out of nowhere then stepped in front of their car, and was now completely blocking the road.

Bill had no choice but to try to escape from it as it peered down at them and, having opened its terrifyingly huge, slavering jaws, filled with hundreds of evil looking spike-like teeth, it gave out a spine-chilling bellowing roar that shook the very air around them as it slowly began to lower its head. Its actions and noise frightened the car's occupants so much they all found themselves nervously shaking. Their car even reverberated from the volume of the gigantic animal's terrifyingly horrendous snarl.

Bill skillfully avoided its first lunge by accelerating across the road just in time and using part of the grass verge to help execute his defensive maneouvre. With blue smoke coming off their car tyres as they did their best to grip the road surface, Bill once again accelerated to get them out of trouble.

The awesome creature again lunged and roared as the smoke from the tyres came up into its face and it just missed their car with its snapping jaws. But sadly that wasn't the end of it.

Another slightly different prehistoric nightmare on legs then jumped in front of their car, forcing Bill to turn left at speed, the car tyres squealing in protest. With smoke pouring out from the car in all directions, Bill managed to heel it over on to just its offside wheels as he turned and skidded into a small car park. The two monsters turned sharply and still roaring at ear-splitting levels, they continued their pursuit. It became all too apparent that both car and creatures were obviously all in the same time zone.

'Leave it to me,' David said, opening his window.

'I wondered when one of you were going to wake up and do something,' Bill sarcastically replied. 'Thanks anyway, Son, but please be quick about it.'

Bill, having reached the end of the car park, had no choice but to reluctantly turn the car to face the creatures, having literally run out of road.

Both monsters then reared simultaneously when they realized they had the car cornered and they both stood perfectly still glowering down at the car and its occupants through evil, glowing, red eyes, saliva dripping from their horrific spiky teeth-filled mouths.

'If it's not too early to panic, this might be a good time,' Mary mused, 'but don't kill them, David.'

'I've no intention of doing that, Sis,' he said, and to everyone's surprise, even Mary's, having removed his seat belt, David stepped out of the car.

'What on earth are you doing, David?' his mum enquired in a high pitched nervous voice.

'They're standing as though they are frozen to the spot and it's obvious they need cooling down a bit,' David said, 'so I'm going to help them do just that.' Then, having pointed his right arm and his now extended index finger at the monsters, he shot out a shimmering blue and white light at both of them. Incredibly, both monsters magically transformed into ice statues. They now really were literally frozen to the spot. David then turned to face the car and his audience with a huge cheeky smile of complete satisfaction on his face.

A split second later, even a loud scream from the three females in the car failed to completely save David as he was roughly grabbed by the slavering jaws of another enormous prehistoric animal which had suddenly and silently materialized between the frozen monsters behind him.

Lunging down, it snapped at his head and fortunately missed, but it did manage to grasp his shoulder with its lips, rather than between its huge and frightening flashing teeth. Having picked David up, the monstrous creature swung him about like a dog shaking a rat. And for David, it hurt like hell.

A sickening thought then flashed into his mind reminding him of the big black and white seagull that had picked up the sand witch on Serpent Dunes Sands beach two years earlier. After firstly shaking and slapping the sand witch about, it had then eaten it!

As he didn't fancy being eaten, David seized the advantage when the creature loosened its grip, trying to get a better purchase on its wriggling captive, and he athletically swung himself up and round on to the back of the head and neck of the animal. Then, repeating what he had done to the other two, he turned the monster he was straddling into an ice statue. He then enjoyed getting down by using the creature's long neck as a convenient slide to return to earth.

'I somehow think Drossmire is going to be a bit pee'd off with us yet again escaping death,' David said, as his dad expertly maneuvered round the frozen monsters and back out on to the road, hoping that now they would be able to reach Tinker's Hall without any more problems. 'I have come to the conclusion that I don't like prehistoric monsters either,' Mary said, having at last found the ability to speak following yet another near death ordeal. 'I don't care if they are supernatural or real, I really don't like them.'

'I think everyone shares your sentiments, Mary,' her mum said, 'they really aren't nice are they?'

'And as for you, young man, let me have a look at your shoulder, it must be very tender.'

'No need to, Mum, thank you,' David said, 'it's fine, and my ankle is too. Our special powers have cured the soreness and pain. Fortunately I'm okay. I'm back to normal.'

'Do you have to be?' Mary joked. Gwen just laughed.

'Wasn't that the site where the Wednesday and Sunday markets and car boot sales are held that we passed a mile or so back near Tonstone, Bill?' Sylvia went on to say.

'And I think I saw a sign for a go-carting course as well,' Arthur said, 'as we had problems this afternoon on the quad bikes it would be great if we could possibly have a session on the go-cart track.'

'Yes, you're both right,' Bill answered. 'Both the markets and go-carting are very popular places for holiday makers as well as locals. We will probably visit one of them, if not both, before we go back home.'

Having arrived at Tinker's Hall car park, Bill found a convenient spot from which to gaze into the grounds. As they quietly looked around what was going to be the focal point of the following afternoon's activities, Sylvia remarked on how peaceful it all appeared to be.

Gwen added, 'But it all might be totally different tomorrow.'

'Well, as I doubt any of it is likely to disappear during the night,' Arthur said, 'I for one will be happy to leave it where it is for now and let's see what tomorrow brings.'

'And I totally agree with Arthur,' Sylvia said, 'let's go back to the cottage for a bit of relaxation. I think everyone has earned it. I don't know about anyone else, but I don't think my nervous system could take any more today.'

'Here, here!' Bill said, 'it's way past the time for us to be having a rest, so we'll go back now and have a bit of tea. Who knows what tomorrow might bring?'

Chapter Twenty

MEDIEVAL JOUSTING DISCUSSED

Back at the cottage they all sat around on the flower-patterned suite enjoying a mug of coffee, sandwiches and cake Sylvia prepared with Mary and Gwen's help. Then they all attempted to make sense of the morning's and especially the afternoon's events. Trying to decide what had been real and what had not wasn't that easy.

'Do I take it that the approval you got to visit "the bunion" was a put up job then, Dad?' David said.

His father replied, 'Yes, Son, I think so.'

'They somehow knew we were going to look at "the bunion",' Mary said, 'so they prepared one of the cannons to shoot at us.'

This time it was Mum who spoke, 'Yes, love, it appears they did know where we were going and what we were going to do.'

'The huge lizards were real enough though,' David said, 'I've got a nasty bruise to prove it, but thankfully it doesn't hurt.' He lifted his leg to show off his big bruise to everyone.

'So you didn't need to phone anyone to apologize for us not keeping our appointment,' Gwen said, 'because no one would have been there to meet us, they only wanted us in the cavern to try and kill us.'

Bill replied, 'No and yes, I think is the answer to that comment, Gwen. But like David and Arthur, I too have a small wound to prove that a number of the scary events were very real.'

'That means that everything that happened at the quad bike centre, before the mechanic came onto the scene that is, was also a set up,' Arthur said. 'But as you said, Mister Knight, my accident and bump on the head were real enough, even if the little girl was possibly only planted in my mind, or did I really see her in front of me?'

David added, 'Yes, that was odd but it prompts another question. Was anyone really hurt in the cave? And what happened to the quad bikes we left out on the trial course, or did we? What I do know is that a female vampire tried to bite Arthur's neck. I didn't imagine that, or at least I don't think I did. But if it was real and if she had managed to bite him, then Arthur would have become a vampire!'

'I don't think I would have liked that,' Arthur replied.

'You probably would have,' David said, 'as you wouldn't have known anything different.'

Arthur just shrugged his shoulders, and Mary caringly squeezed his hand.

'I really hated what happened on the way back from Cliffthorpe Bay too,' Sylvia said, 'those prehistoric creatures were really frightening. I don't think I have ever been as scared, even when we were confronted with the first and smelly presence of that obnoxious Offalmire two years ago.'

'And that was scary enough,' Mary said.

'One good thing about all of today's action,' Bill said, 'is that it all took place in our own magical parallel time slot. It didn't and couldn't affect ordinary people enjoying their holidays or going about their normal everyday lives.'

'There really aren't any red-eyed entities lurking about anywhere, or lizards that might grow big or prehistoric animal statues that might come to life, it's just in our supernatural time that these things occur. But I'm still not exactly sure how much of what happened today did only happen in our minds.'

'I'm not sure what happened in your mind, Dad,' David said, 'but I know my ankle and my shoulder are bruised even though they no longer hurt. I can assure you I didn't only imagined that they hurt. So, what else has Drossmire got up his devious evil sleeve? And if you say a devious evil arm, Sis, I'll hit you with mine.'

They all enjoyed David's quip which helped relax the obvious tension they were still experiencing.

'So, as tomorrow is the day of the main event,' Bill said, 'let's try and clear our minds of this day's happenings and focus our thoughts on tomorrow.'

'I'll make something for tea,' Sylvia said, 'you five can start to prepare a positive action plan rather than just chatting about it.'

'Mum's right though,' David said, 'we really do need to decide what we are going to do and make a list of anything we might need that we don't already have. I think we, me and Sis, are now capable of using our supernatural powers to produce just about anything we might need. Being able to become invisible just when we wanted to this afternoon has convinced me of that.'

'I didn't see that,' Bill said jokingly.

'Me neither,' Arthur remarked more seriously.

'You were in no state to see anything at the time it was all happening,' David said. 'Anyway, you were invisible at the time as well,' Arthur just looked shocked.

'Sis and I will have a go at contacting Merlin after tea, to get some idea what he has in his mind. Knowing that will help us to further develop anything we come up with.'

Mary agreed, saying it would be nice to have a chat with him again anyway.

Once the tea things had been tidied and the pots washed and cleared away, everyone sat round on the three-piece suite to discuss and start to formulate the following day's basic action plan.

'Merlin said he had let Drossmire know through one of his Other World beings,' David said, 'that we would be going to Tinker's Hall to have a bit of fun staging some mock fighting events.'

'And that should be of great interest to Drossmire as he is an enthusiast of jousting, even though a coward himself!' Merlin said, having appeared in the room behind Bill's chair and making everybody jump.

'You've done it again, Merlin,' Sylvia said, 'you have surprised everyone by arriving literally out of thin air.'

'I am most sorry, Sylvia, I have no wish to alarm or shock any of you, but it just seemed an appropriate time for me to join the discussions.'

'It's a perfect time, Merlin, and thank you for joining us,' Bill said, 'your input will be most appreciated.'

'Dad had already told us about the ghost of the white lady and the tortured alligator, and that Tinker's Hall was the venue for many medieval jousting contests,' Mary said, 'but it appears some of our knowledge of parts of the jousting scene is a little bit sketchy to say the least.'

'Well allow me to enlighten you,' Merlin said, removing the magazines and newspapers from the coffee table.

He then, by using his supernatural abilities, astounded everyone by creating miniature people, horses, railings, fences, tents, bunting, flags and a host of other things which he magically made appear on the table. He then astonished the already gob-smacked six even more when, from and using the assembled live miniature figures, he set up a real medieval tournament scene. The six would-be jousting participants now looked on totally mesmerized.

'You, Sylvia, and Bill, along with the twins are experts in the martial arts which are practised in modern times,' Merlin said. 'Jousting contests were a form of and a variety of martial arts using the weapons which were applicable to those times, and which started as far back as 1066. The skills demonstrated by contestants in such tournaments were simply recreations of those needed to enable them to win contests in real battles and warfare.'

At that moment two miniature armour clad figures which had been standing on the table began a sword fight using heavy swords, and their skills were amazing.

Merlin then continued. 'Archery contests were always popular at such events,' and the two swordsmen disappeared and were replaced by ranks of archers, some with long bows, others with crossbows. 'It was possible for skillful knights and other contestants to make much money, but sadly many lost their lives or suffered terrible wounds in some of the events.'

Two knights on horseback then appeared on the table carrying lances and charging at speed in opposite directions separated by a fence, the archers having disappeared.

Merlin then went on to say, 'The fence between the contestants who are jousting is called a tilt. Those competing on horseback are practising what is known as tilting. The lances they use are blunt and only used to unseat their opponents, enabling the contest to continue on foot using hand weapons of their choice, and the area in which a tournament takes place, like that grassed area in front of Tinker's Hall, is named a tiltyard.'

Everything then disappeared from the table and there was a silence for about six seconds which you could have cut with a knife as the audience of six desperately tried to absorb everything the magical miniature people had so skillfully demonstrated to them on the coffee table, thanks to Merlin's capabilities.

David, as he often did, was first to speak. 'Wow! That was some explanation and demonstration, Merlin. I know I speak for everyone when I say thank you so much for all that. It really was brillfanmagical.'

'Yes, David, I must agree with you,' Merlin said, and he laughed. 'It was, as you said, brillfanmagical.' And everyone laughed at that. 'But one thing I failed to mention was that all the tournaments are concerned with honour. A code of chivalry must prevail and be demonstrated in all the events or they mean absolutely nothing, and the spectators will be very upset and demonstrate their displeasure. I think it could be considered as being similar to a yellow or red card in some of your inflated ball sports and pastimes.' And Merlin's comments again brought a big grin to the faces of the six observers' nodding heads.

'Our thanks again, Merlin,' Bill said, 'apart from demonstrating some of our own type of martial arts fighting, we can now also choose which other ones we might consider having a go at, but at the same time not forgetting what the main event has to be.'

'Yes,' said Merlin, 'since I last spoke with you Red has informed me that there has been a lot of unwelcome activity from Drossmire and his henchmen at Moatcaster Castle, and I fear he is almost ready to access the Crystal Tower to steal and misuse the Thirteen Treasures of Britain. That must be prevented from happening, whatever the cost.'

'I am more than sorry to have to put it to you like that, Sylvia, but it really is that important! Good luck tomorrow! I will not be far away and may the good wishes of the Gods of the Terrestrial Light be with you!' And he disappeared.

'That was something else, wasn't it?' Mary said.

'It is truly remarkable what Merlin can do,' Arthur said, 'he is such a competent wizard.'

'Oddly enough, I don't think of him as a wizard,' Sylvia said, 'to me he's just Merlin. That's probably because he's in our family tree. He's just one of us.'

'He's got to be a bit special though hasn't he?' Gwen said. 'I wish he was in our tree.'

'Let's branch our thoughts off at that point, Gwen,' David said grinning, 'I don't think we can do much more tonight, so let's whisk Arthur and Gwen back in their car to their aunty's house, Sis. Later you and I can have that chat I know you are dying to have with me.'

Mary agreed and they all said goodnight before David and Mary whisked the other twins off into the start of a gorgeous glowing orange sunset.

After saying goodnight to Arthur and Gwen with a kiss each on the cheek, they secured their aunty's house with a magical protective shield to ensure there would be no problems for either of them in the night. Then, having flown back to their holiday cottage, they increased the shield on their own building before they went into Mary's bedroom for the discussion she knew David wanted to have about tomorrow…

Chapter Twenty One

THE TWINS LOSE THEIR POWERS

All of the Knight family had a restless night, thinking about what might happen when they got to Tinker's Hall. The thought of meeting up again with the repulsive and evil Drossmire was enough to put them off going, but they knew they had to, and were all prepared to meet and face him to be able to carry out their responsibilities.

It was a beautiful morning and the weather was perfect for an outdoor event. David helped his dad to wash their car while Mary and her mum got out clean sets of their favourite seven magpies black strip. Looking a good team was almost as important to them as fighting well, and they were all looking forward to wearing their magpie strip for the main event. Sylvia also made sure their bum bags were laid out ready to wear.

They had arranged to pick up Arthur and Gwen at 9.15 a.m. so they could all travel together and arrive at Tinker's Hall a little after 10.00 o'clock, which was when the hall normally opened to visitors. This wasn't going to bother them though, as Merlin had created a particularly special portal into a parallel time, allowing them to have the full run of the hall and its grounds to themselves.

The sun was shining brightly in a beautiful azure blue sky and the few small cotton wool clouds helped to set the scene. It was a perfect day and they all hoped it might stay that way.

'I think I'll leave the car in the main car park,' Bill said having done the chauffeuring, 'we can then walk in to have a good look round before we commit ourselves to anything.'

Having looked at all they could see from the outside, they decided that going in now made sense. Understandably feeling a little apprehensive, in they went.

They first walked round the lake and had a close look at the boathouse. Their noses then helped them sniff round the herb garden and lastly the beautiful rose gardens. Their investigative walk then took them further into the grounds via the archway of the mock gatehouse which had been built into the outer garden wall. The path then led across a wide grassed area towards the arch of the second gatehouse in the inner wall.

The side of the hall's east wing, which was coated with a growth of ivy, was also almost totally covered with scaffolding while some restoration work was underway on the window frames, and it gave the hall a somewhat cloaked and eerie look.

'I feel we don't need to go into the building or much further at the moment,' David said, 'in fact my senses are telling me to consider going back.'

'Mine too, Bruv,' Mary said agreeing with David, 'I somehow feel we need to be outside the hall, but I don't know where the message is coming from.'

A gap had occurred between each couple after they had left the rose gardens as some of them had loitered smelling at the roses. David and Mary were about ten paces in front of their mum and dad who were the middle couple. Arthur and Gwen were bringing up the rear about another ten yards or so behind. Suddenly so much seemed alarmingly to start to happen. As David and Mary walked into and under the arch of the garden's inner wall mock gatehouse, the first terrible and horrendous event occurred.

A huge deluge of water cascaded down through the five holes in the roof, which are known as murder holes, and totally soaked David and Mary who were passing under them.

The terrible and specific thing about the event was that the Terrestrial Twins' supernatural powers had once more been cleverly and, sadly effectively, short-circuited. From past experiences the twins were aware that, whilst wet, their powers were dramatically reduced or even temporarily removed. But even worse, Drossmire had somehow added a devious magical element to the water and, as a consequence, the twins were temporarily unable to move their feet. They were helplessly stuck where they were.

Drossmire had obviously known the facts about water and created an ambush to soak and effectively weaken the twins. The only skills and strengths they had left were their own. But they were unable to move to use them.

At the same time as the twins were getting their drenching, two of Drossmire's thugs materialized from nowhere behind Bill and Sylvia and, before they realized what was happening, they were sadly both knocked to the ground, unconscious.

The terrible form of Drossmire himself then appeared behind them, having observed that his dirty work had been done for him. He bent down and easily picked up the twins' parents, one under each arm as he was a tall, powerfully built figure. He then turned and annoyingly brushed past the inert David and Mary and walked towards the east wing of the hall carrying their parents with him.

Mary was distraught but there was nothing David could do this time to console his sister, rooted as he was to the spot. Instead they both just stood there, dripping wet and quite woozy, desperately trying to re-orientate and focus their minds.

Meanwhile, Arthur and Gwen were shocked and dismayed by the two events they had just witnessed, having observed both of the ambushes. They too were now desperately trying to decide what might be the best thing to do having once again been so suddenly and horrendously plunged into such seemingly unbelievable circumstances.

David made their minds up for them when he realized the two fiends who had just floored his parents were menacingly approaching he and Mary, murder in their eyes. And he shouted to Arthur and Gwen to get out of the grounds of the hall now while they could. They would deal with Drossmire's morons themselves.

'Go, get out while you can. We'll contact and meet up with you later after we've dealt with these thugs!'

David and Mary then thankfully felt the strength returning to their legs and feet. They were now almost ready to face their attackers, but they both were really surprised and a little disappointed to see them suddenly disappear. They had simply vanished. So David and Mary set off in the direction in which their parents had been taken, the east wing of the hall.

They had only just emerged from the gatehouse arch when there was the most unpleasant sound of arrows whistling through the air, then thud, thud. Horrendously both David and Mary had received a crossbow dart in the chest, and down they went...

Having fallen, they lay on the path, motionless...

Chapter Twenty Two

THE KNIGHTS FIGHT EACH OTHER

'That was a good idea of yours, Sis, for us all to wear protective vests under our shirts,' David whispered from the side of his mouth as they lay on the path facing each other. 'They really saved us from those crossbow arrows.'

'We women have over the years learned to think about the importance of safety, Bruv,' Mary replied, with a slight smile on her now dirty face where the dust on the path had stuck to her wet cheeks. 'Drossmire's morons will probably take us in if we lay still and pretend to be dead.'

Barely a minute had passed before the two thugs reappeared and having roughly picked them up, carried the twins, not into the building, but into a corner of the courtyard where they were unceremoniously dumped.

The twins allowed their captors to go back into the building before doing anything. Having found that he still had limited, though weakened, telepathic abilities, David used them to contact Red. Earlier, before leaving the cottage, they had asked Red to be at Tinker's Hall just in case they needed his services.

Red replied to say that he was sitting on top of the first gatehouse, but was glad he was invisible as all sorts of things were happening out in front of him.

David apologized to Red for ignoring what he was trying to tell him as he desperately needed to talk to him, and Red understood once David told him what had happened; that he needed him to come as quickly as possible to breathe some warm air on to he and Mary and help them to dry off more quickly. Red realized that their supernatural powers and abilities would return once they dried out.

Having located Mary and David, Red only partially materialized so as not to be so readily seen, then commenced blowing warm air across them.

'Whatever have you been eating, Red?' was the question Mary put to him once she felt his warm breath flood across her.

'I don't think you really want to know, Mary,' was Red's questionable reply, so she thought it best that she didn't press him for more information.

David's idea worked, and it wasn't long before he and Mary were totally dry again and thankfully in full possession of all of their special supernatural powers. They both thanked Red for his help and he disappeared.

A few minutes later Drossmire's two thugs returned to the twins who, having decided it was best to continue playing dead, allowed themselves to be carried into the building and on into the kitchen of the Hall. They were again dumped into another corner, this time on top of each other, Mary on top.

'I can read your mind don't forget, Sis, and no, you're all right, I'm not going to move it,' David said grinning to himself about his sister's slight embarrassment.

The twins were then horrified to see that although their parents had recovered from the attack they had been securely and uncomfortably lashed to the tops of two wooden tables.

Standing close to the head end of the tables and towering above them was the ugly and menacing figure of Drossmire. He had been annoyingly bragging to their parents at the same time as the twins were taken into the kitchen and dumped in the corner.

'I now have the bodies of your two precious Terrestrial Twins,' and he gave out a horrible sickly laugh. The sound echoed weirdly round the huge, vaulted stone-walled room. 'And I have to say, they have been a very big disappointment to me. They proved to be far easier to kill than I thought they would be. I really expected them to be much more capable adversaries than they proved to be. I had anticipated that they would have been a lot more competitive and I wanted them to die slowly and painfully. But, as I now have you, I suppose you two will have to do.

'First of all I will enjoy drinking some of the blood from your necks to weaken you. I will then sit on your chests so you can't breathe, that way you will both die a most horrific and painful death. I will then have reaped my retribution for the death of my father.'

That, David decided, was enough. He had already heard far too much and he literally flew at Drossmire, belting him with an expertly placed double footed kick on the side of his head, which must have hurt like hell and sent Drossmire sprawling. For a brief moment expressions of shock, pain, horror and disbelief flitted across Drossmire's face before he literally disappeared. David and Mary then, having ripped off their parents' bindings, lovingly hugged each of them as they sat up.

'Thank God neither of you is really dead,' Sylvia said and started to cry, as the total shock and stress of the experience mingled with the relief and pleasure of seeing her children alive again. Mary helped her climb off the table andBill took her in his arms and held her while he explained what Drossmire's men had told them; how they had shot their twins with crossbow arrows. 'You were right about us all needing to wear protective vests, Mary,' her dad said, 'it really did prove to be a very worthwhile precaution didn't it?'

'And I wouldn't tell you what she said to me even if you paid me,' David joked at Mary's expense, but she just glowered at him.

'Oh, and thanks for saving your Mum and me yet again. We were only unconscious for a short time, and apart from a bit of a bump on the head and we're used to receiving those, we're both all right. Do you think you two saving or rescuing us is becoming a habit?'

'If it is, Dad, you're very welcome, you'll both just have to get used to it I suppose,' replied David. 'But no more talk for now, Dad. We're both okay as well, but we've no idea what has happened to Gwen and Arthur. When Red came to dry us, he said something about there being lots of things happening, but I've no idea what he meant or what the *things* might be.'

No, none of them were aware of the other things that had happened, and they were odd to say the least!

Arthur, who was a few paces ahead of Gwen, was amazed when he emerged from the arch of the gatehouse to find his clothing had magically been changed to that of a well to do medieval person. Also, and seemingly out of thin air, the field in front of him had incredibly transformed into the very busy scene of a tiltyard. The whole area now contained the fences and staging necessary for a variety of events including jousting tournaments. There were tents, bunting, flags and people busying themselves everywhere preparing equipment and weapons and setting up targets. It looked just as Merlin had shown them on the table in miniature the night before.

Gwen was delayed for a second or two as she had to stand with her back to the wall at the other side of the arch to allow a group of children in medieval dress to pass her, busying themselves chasing after a number of geese.

A caller, standing on the edge of the tiltyard and dressed as a jester, and who had been announcing visitors' names, turned and having spotted Arthur asked him for his name so that he could announce him.

'Er, Arthur, I'm Arthur.'

Arthur then turned to Gwen, who was also gob-smacked as she admired the beautiful, high quality, long, pale blue medieval dress that had magically appeared on her body. He beckoned her to come out from under the arch and stand with him. He tried his best to shout to her above the noise of the crowd who were cheering at a couple who were sword fighting. 'HERE! GWEN OVER 'ERE!'

The jester, who was also experiencing the same problem of not been able to hear because of the excited shouting of the crowds, then turned towards the centre of the tiltyard arena and in an extraordinarily loud voice shouted what he felt sure was what he had heard Arthur say....

'PRAY SILENCE! I NOW HAVE THE HONOUR OF PRESENTING,'.... he paused to clear his throat then really surprised everyone by announcing..... 'ARTHUR AND GUINEVERE!'

The arena suddenly went very quiet... Seconds later, there was a huge cheer and applause from the crowd as Arthur and Gwen were escorted to two chairs in the centre of a platform positioned in front of a medium-sized pale blue tent. It rather looked like they had unwittingly become the guests of honour.

'What's happened, Arthur?' Gwen asked in a puzzled and surprised voice.

'I have no idea,' was Arthur's answer. 'There seems to be some sort of jousting tournament taking place. The whole tiltyard and everything you can see amazingly materialized as I emerged from under the arch. It appears we are being treated like royalty, even though as a couple we physically look very different to them. You have shortish white hair and mine is even shorter and black as a raven, whereas most of the crowd had much longer brown hair. It all seems a bit odd. But as we've got the best two seats in the house, what the heck does it matter? To be honest, Gwen, I don't even know whether or not we're in the same time-slot any more!'

'But what are we going to do about the others, David and Mary and their mum and mad?' Gwen remarked.

'I feel confident they will be able to reach us wherever they are when they want to,' Arthur replied. 'And as we can't do a thing about it at the moment, I suggest we simply enjoy what is happening.'

Targets made from bales of straw were being placed ready for a longbow archery contest which was well received by the enthusiastic crowd when it got underway, as they really appreciated the amazing levels of skill and ability being demonstrated.

The contest was eventually won by an archer dressed mainly in green. When he came forward to collect his prize money, he leaned into the pavilion and speaking to Arthur and Gwen said, 'Tell the Knight family I enjoyed meeting and helping them two years ago, and I am sorry I did not see them on this occasion, perhaps another time.' Arthur and Gwen just looked blankly at each other and shrugged their shoulders having no idea who the archer was.

The caller then made a new announcement. 'WE NOW HAVE FOUR KNIGHTS BEARING THE ARMS OF SEVEN MAGPIES... ONE OF THE YOUNG ONES HAS CALLED THE EVENT 'BRILLFANMAGICAL!'

A huge cheer and round of applause then erupted from the crowd as Bill, closely followed by Sylvia, David and Mary, entered the tiltyard arena through the same gatehouse arch. They were all looking particularly impressive in their black magpie strip which they had magically cleaned.

Robin Hood, for he was the one who had won the archery tournament, and whose poisoned arrows helped kill King Offalmire two years earlier, then asked the caller to announce that the four would give a demonstration, a friendly fight, using the martial skills in which they were experts. And he did!

To then see David and Mary along with their parents giving a demonstration of their expert martial arts skills was a sight to behold. Obviously no one in the medieval crowd had ever witnessed anything quite like it and they loved it. They really appreciated all of the fighting and defensive skills being demonstrated to them by two more different looking couples, two more with black hair and two whose hair was virtually white.

Suddenly a huge bellowing roar echoed round the tiltyard arena and the grotesque shape of Drossmire magically appeared close to the pavilion, making both Arthur and Gwen, and the young pages assisting them with the prize-giving, duck back as far away from him as the side and back of the tent allowed.

Drossmire then totally amazed everybody by suddenly turning emerald green from head to toe. The little bits and tufts of hair he had on his head then weirdly grew and grew until they resembled a green floor mop. He looked absolutely ridiculous and the crowd, which had gone very quiet when he appeared, slowly began to snigger. The sniggering then grew louder and louder as it built to a crescendo and rippled round the tiltyard until everyone was laughing their heads off at him.

Drossmire, who had obviously intended to frighten everyone by becoming green, now looked utterly ridiculous. His idea had totally backfired on him. Being laughed at by the large crowd, whom he had intended to frighten, really infuriated him and he shook with rage, which made him look even more ridiculous. He now looked like an ugly, bloated mass of quivering green jelly.

Seeing Offalmire shaking so ridiculously with rage pleased the Knight family even more than just laughing at him, and along with the loudly jeering crowd they all enjoyed being part of the fun.

Drossmire then bellowed out a challenge. 'Who will be man enough, big enough and brave enough to face me? Who will challenge me, the magnificent Drossmire? I am now fighting as the Green Knight. Who amongst you will be bold enough to dare to challenge me in a contest of skill and honour?'

There was silence for a few seconds and you could have heard a pin drop, no one daring to speak. Then, without any warning and before either David or his sister could say anything, every person in the tiltyard was suddenly taken aback with complete surprise, particularly Drossmire, when out of a black and white tent at the far end of the tiltyard area emanated a rich, loud, booming manly voice. 'I, Sir, will accept your pathetic challenge, and do so on behalf of the Knight family and their friends.'

Then, out of the tent, and to a tumultuous roaring cheer and enthusiastic applause, riding a magnificent glossy coated black stallion covered in black and white striped drapes, rode a knight in black and white light armour. The black and white flag fluttering on the end of his blunt lance and his black shield was displaying Bill's seven magpies business logo as its coat of arms. With a crest of black and white magpie feathers on his helmet, he looked absolutely magnificent!

'I'd know that voice anywhere,' Sylvia said rather excitedly, 'it's Sir Gawain. He's turned up to help us again like he did two years ago and to represent us in the tournament as our own special knight. I think he's wonderful, don't you, Bill?'

Bill replied saying, 'Yes, love, he really is a great guy.'

'Wasn't it Sir Gawain who accepted the Green Knight's challenge in the legendary King Arthur's Court event and then chopped his head off?' remarked Mary turning to Bill.

'Yes, love, you're right, and it looks like they are going to re-live what was known as the beheading game. If Sir Gawain wins and does cut off Drossmire's head, he will have terminated him for us. I wonder if the Gods of the Terrestrial Light are behind him being here to do that for us. However, if he loses, he will be in real danger of having his own head removed.'

'But Sir Gawain is already dead, Dad, he's a ghost,' Mary said, 'we know he's a friendly one, but he is still a ghost and he is most certainly already very dead.'

Sylvia smiling had the answer, 'Well, in that case, we'll just not bother to tell Drossmire then eh, love?'

Drossmire looked totally taken aback by the fact that someone had actually accepted his challenge to fight, and backed up as far as he could as Sir Gawain trotted closer to him. As he reached him Sir Gawain fully raised the visor on his helmet then just laughed out loud at Drossmire, who looked a poor excuse for a knight. And the crowd joined in with the laughter.

Drossmire looked angry enough to burst, but did the opposite. He magically managed to squeeze himself into the suit of green armour which his squires had brought out for him from his green striped tent.

'We are all aware you like a tournament and spectacle, Drossmire,' Sir Gawain said in a serious voice, 'but you must remember this is a contest of honour. A spirit of chivalry must prevail throughout the engagement. It must be an honorable fight in all quarters of the event.'

There was an eerie calm then as the crowd remained totally silent during Sir Gawain's presentation and the laying down of the terms of their ensuing tournament.

Sir Gawain then went on to say, 'You may or may not know, but I cut off the head of the Green Knight in King Arthur's Court and, if I win, I will be very happy to remove yours.' He then, by expertly using his reins, and accompanied by raptures applause and cheers from the crowd, turned his horse and trotted back to his tent to prepare himself for the encounter…

Chapter Twenty Three

THE MAIN AND FINAL EVENT

The tilt fence was checked and the two contestants prepared themselves at their respective ends of the arena.

Arthur was asked to lower the sword, which he found on a shelf under the table in front of him, to start the contest. The horns were then sounded for battle to commence!

It was only when Sir Gawain felt and heard the lance being used by Drossmire scratch the shoulder of his armour as they passed each other on what was supposed to be a presentation and warm-up run, not part of the actual challenge engagement, that he realized Drossmire was cheating. He was using a metal and sharp-tipped lance, not the blunt wooden one which he should have been carrying. But as Sir Gawain expertly succeeded in knocking Drossmire's shield from his hand on their next and first proper competitive run, he was really looking forward to the second.

They had almost reached each other on that second run, when Sir Gawain's acute hearing made him aware of two crossbow arrows winging their way towards his head. He ducked skillfully to avoid them. However, as the darts had failed to hit their target, they carried on through the air and embedded themselves in the chests of two more of Drossmire's archers who were preparing to shoot at him from the other side of the tiltyard. The assembled crowd had seen what had happened and they really annoyed

Drossmire, who was almost unseated by his horse, when they spontaneously and loudly cheered as both of his archers fell dead from the raised staging on which they had been standing.

Sir Gawain was so enraged by Drossmire's blatant and unchivalrous behaviour that he rode close enough to the tilt fence to be able to thrust his arm out, fisting Drossmire in the face and knocking him from his saddle. Drossmire then tightly grabbed hold of his horse's green drapes in a futile attempt to straighten-up but failed to do so and still went flying off his horse, to a tremendous cheer from the now very excited crowd.

Next the two contestants were to face each other on foot using battle axes, which had been their choice of weapon. The hand axe being one of Sir Gawain's favourite weapons.

All of the magpie team were surprised that Drossmire had wanted to fight at all, as Merlin had told them he was a coward, yet here he was fighting for his life. Or was he? Was this really Drossmire or had he somehow conjured up someone or something else to fight for him.

They were soon to find out, for when Sir Gawain brought his axe down on his opponent's neck, having floored him with three mighty blows of his axe, his helmet shot off. But there was no head inside!

The crowd groaned in both surprise and disappointment. But just as they started to shout their disapproval, there was a terrific blinding green flash, and the whole of the jousting tiltyard with everyone and everything in it disappeared, including Sir Gawain. Our six intrepid heroes were left standing in what now, apart from them, was a totally empty field. They had yet again been fooled by Drossmire.

'Did that really happen, or did we imagine it?' David questioned.

'Oh! I think it happened, Son', was his dad's reply.

A magpie then appeared on Bill's shoulder and after congratulating all of them for putting on such a splendid display in the tiltyard, went on to say that Merlin had sent him to inform them where Drossmire was.

Still in a raging temper, he had returned to the kitchens of the Hall. Along with his helpers, he was apparently now busy setting up six tables on which he intended to individually tether each of them.

'I think we need to surprise him if we are going to find a way of getting rid of him today,' David said, 'and I think I know how to do it.'

'Let's all go back into the courtyard. Mary and I will then make ourselves invisible. That way we should be able to sneak into the Hall undetected and find a way of finishing him off, bearing in mind he might have a protective shield round him. We'll just have to play it by ear so to speak. You four can be our back-up outside.'

David and Mary had just become invisible before going into the Hall when there was a terrible scream from Gwen. A huge alligator, unseen by any of them, had suddenly appeared in the wide stream behind them which ran down to the lake. Having reached up out of the water it had managed to snatch hold of Gwen. Being so powerful and covered in tough scales, it totally ignored her thumping and kicking. Having quickly slipped its body back into the water and at remarkable speed it headed for the lake. Fortunately for Gwen, the stream wasn't deep enough for the monstrous creature to completely submerge, so Gwen's head was clear of the water. Still punching and kicking, she disappeared out of sight having been taken under a humped-back stone bridge where the path to the Hall went over the stream.

The terrifying scaly creature was the ghost of the tortured alligator that haunted the lake in the grounds of the Hall. Drossmire had somehow managed to get it to do some of his evil dirty work.

Fortunately for Gwen, one of the heartless and unbelievably cruel things the alligator's evil tinker owner had done to it when he had tortured it, was to enjoy breaking its jaw with a crowbar which had left a curve in it when it healed. He'd also pulled out most of its teeth, leaving only the long ones at the front of its jaws. As Gwen was so slim and the creature had grasped her in the centre of its jaws, she wasn't being gripped too tightly and fortunately also had not been bitten.

However, her screams had alerted Drossmire's thugs to their presence and six of them came dashing out to investigate. Two of them then received the surprise of their lives when they were first lifted off the ground and spun round before being knocked about by their invisible attackers. Finally, they were zapped and dissolved into the usual slimy mucus pools the twins had become all too familiar with.

The other two thugs were easily floored after a short fight with Arthur and Bill, one of them having first received a nasty kick where it really hurts from Sylvia when he foolishly rushed at her.

'He might not have been a farmer,' Bill jokingly naughtily said, 'but he's certainly got two acres now.'

The last two were then dealt with in the same way as the first pair. But sadly and annoyingly the cowardly, obnoxious Drossmire was nowhere to be seen. He had disappeared.

Merlin, as usual, didn't fail to surprise them when he suddenly appeared, materializing close to Arthur and said,

'Don't worry, young man, I feel sure we will soon have your sister back.'

Merlin then went on to say, 'First of all, David and Mary, I will telepathically send a message to the alligator.'

'But what if he doesn't take any notice of your message?' Sylvia said, now sounding very concerned. 'What if it takes her into the lake and she drowns?'

'If I thought that were to happen, Sylvia, I would expect the twins to fly to the lake and save her.'

'Thanks a lot, Merlin!' David, Mary and Arthur said together.

At that moment they were all slightly taken by surprise as the terrifying sight of the hulking shape of the obnoxious Drossmire came roaring out of the Hall, stopping just outside the doorway, his huge ugly frame totally blocking the entrance. What amazed everyone was not the fact that he had come out to face them, but that in his right hand he was surprisingly holding a magnificent gleaming and jewel-hilted sword.

'You can now all quiver and shake with fear,' he confidently announced to them. 'None of you knew I was successful in my search for the thing my father failed to find, Arthur's sword, Excalibur!' And he waved the sword above his head then pointed it at them. 'I now am invincible. I cannot be beaten or killed by anyone, especially you measly set of gutless mortals. It now is time to dispose of all of you. I have tired of playing games with you. Prepare yourselves to die a painful death.'

'I for one don't think so,' Arthur said in a very strong and forceful voice which stopped Drossmire in his tracks. 'Excalibur was made for Arthur, and as I am the only person here who has that name, I, Sir, rightly claim the sword as mine.' And having stepped closer to Drossmire, he held out his hand in the direction of the sword.

The reaction of the sword was instant as was the shock experienced by everyone, particularly Drossmire who screamed in pain, anger and fear as the sword, having painfully ripped itself from his grasp, astonished everyone when it shot through the air to where Arthur's outstretched right hand was waiting to receive it.

Noticing that Drossmire wasn't protected by a safety shield, Arthur said, 'Who is it who now trembles in fear, Drossmire?' Continuing with a huge grin on his face he said, 'It's certainly not us, but it does look an awful lot like it might be you!' He then began to walk slowly and purposely towards Drossmire, making gentle circular movements with the point of the sword whilst pointing it at his nether regions. Drossmire then quite involuntarily wet his pants as he stood frighteningly rooted to the spot, visibly shaking, his pee running down his ugly, scaly legs and into, and filling, his deer hide boots!

It then was Merlin's turn to surprise everyone, including Drossmire, by walking past Arthur and straight up to the now very subdued ugly, evil being. He then totally amazed everyone even more when, after raising his right hand and pointing his index finger at Drossmire, he said, 'You, the evil one, no longer have a place on this terrestrial planet, this Earth. I have just been informed that you wanted to be the owner of this fine Tinker's Hall here at Crossthorpe. Well, the Gods of the Terrestrial Light have also informed me that for a short time your wish to become the owner is to be granted.

'However, it will be in the form of one of its previous owners, a tinker who gave the Hall its name. He was the man who brought some alligators here and chained up the biggest one and who tormented and was extremely cruel to it. He even sadistically tortured it. The mythological story also says that the evil tinker perished in a fire along with the alligator after it had managed to inflict its retribution on him. You, Drossmire, are now to become that evil man!'

With a fearful and terrified expression on his face, the huge shape of the obnoxious Drossmire slowly began to change as he steadily reduced in size, shape and appearance until he had transformed into the physical image of the alligator's cruel tinker owner. Even his clothes changed to the type of period clothing worn in the seventeenth century by the legendary, evil owner of Tinker's Hall.

'Wow!' Mary said, 'I sense that Drossmire is soon going to be feeling even more unhappy than he does now, if that's possible.'

After turning towards the twins, Merlin then went on to say, 'I have telepathically beamed a message to the alligator to not go into the lake, but to head for the boathouse. He will realise it has come from me and will carry out my request. The rest will be up to you, David and Mary, when you understand the meaning of a message you are about to receive from a visitor, the White Lady.'

Meanwhile, we must transport Drossmire down to the lake, I am sure the alligator will release Gwen as soon as it sees him. You will then have her back in your company, David, and I know that will please you greatly.'

As Merlin finished speaking, Drossmire, now looking the image of the legendary tinker owner, was amazingly lifted about a foot from the pebbled surface of the courtyard by an invisible supernatural force. He then helplessly began moving through the air at walking pace following the path leading to the lake. His terrified struggling was doing him no good at all, and the best word to describe the look on his face was tortured. Drossmire was in deep trouble and could only do two things about it – nothing and fizz all!

Then the figure of an attractive lady in a long white dress surprised them all when she materialised in front of them. It was the friendly ghost of the White Lady.

'You do not have much time, David and Mary,' she said, 'but I know you have realised that of the many things Drossmire is, one of them is a vampire, which means he can be killed by supernatural fire.' Having imparted her message, she smiled and vanished as quickly as she had arrived.

'She's absolutely right,' David said as he grabbed Mary's hand, a thoughtful expression on his face, as both he and Mary at the same time now realised the meaning behind the message. Then together they took off and quickly flew out of the courtyard in the direction of the lake.

As their feet lifted from the floor, David telepathically contacted Red. 'Are you still on the top of the gatehouse, Red?'

'Yes, David, and I can see Drossmire. Do you want me stop him?'

'No thanks, Red,' David replied, 'but I would like you to go over to the boathouse.'

The twins then landed alongside Red who had just materialized near the side of the boathouse having again become visible. 'Just walk to the edge of the path with us, Red,' David said. 'All we want you to do is to divert Drossmire from the footpath and make him go up the stairs and into what was once the storeroom above the boathouse.' So Red obliged.

Drossmire breathlessly ran the last one hundred and fifty yards towards the boathouse having been lowered to the path by the tractor beam and having received a mental message from the White Lady that the boathouse may be a safe place for him to go to escape.

He only had a few more yards to go but was gasping for breath, his lungs feeling like they would burst with pain as Merlin had magically made his shoes feel like concrete weights, making the last few dozen yards feel like the end of a gruelling marathon.

He finally reached the point when he was confronted by the dragon's tail and the huge scaled bulk of Red's body. His path was totally blocked. The position of Red's body now forced Drossmire to move to his left, not only nearer to the boathouse but also, sadly for him, closer to the lake.

The ghost alligator which had turned to see what all the noise was about, couldn't believe its eyes or its luck. For there, and standing only a few yards from it, was the one person in the world which it totally hated. It was the tinker! And having dropped Mary onto the grass next to the path, the now enraged alligator gave out a blood curdling roar that echoed round the lake and it started to waddle towards Drossmire. Its speed increasing at each step it made.

Drossmire, shaking with fright from head to toe, again involuntary wet himself as he set off heading for the steps up to the boathouse's storeroom, the angry alligator now moving in the same direction terrifyingly bellowing and roaring with every step it took.

Drossmire, now even more breathless than before and also belching and breaking wind every few difficult steps he took, struggled up the boathouse steps. Exhausted, he painfully heaved his weighted feet and aching legs up the last of the stairs and virtually fell into the small room. He was then closely followed by the insanely angry and furiously roaring ghost alligator, retribution being the only thought on its inflamed and tortured mind and soul.

As Drossmire's painful screams and the roars of the alligator filled the air around them, David asked Red if he would breathe fire in through the window.

'I can do better than that, David,' Red replied, 'I took the liberty of inviting my mate, Snowy, my white dragon friend, to watch the jousting when it started, and he's still here. He can blast through the window on the other side, as he just happens to be sitting over there at this very moment.

Both dragons then reared up to stand on their hind legs and to get their mouths and nostrils close to the windows, and both belched out roaring flames for about half of a minute. As soon as the dragon flamethrowers started the noises from inside stopped instantly.

Once the dragons were satisfied they had magically done enough, they stopped belching flames and lowered themselves to place their four feet on the ground.

'The alligator ghost will have gone back into the lake, no worse for wear,' Red said, 'but Drossmire will now be nothing more than cindered ash. Nothing can escape the supernatural power of our flames once they are targeted.'

'He is absolutely correct. The dragons did a splendid job terminating Drossmire's existence,' Merlin said, having just arrived on the scene and having transported Bill, Sylvia, Arthur and Gwen with him.

The twins could see that Arthur was no longer in possession of the sword Excalibar, Merlin having magically returned it to Lilymire Lake from where it had been found.

Merlin then went on to say, 'Thank you, Red, and your friend Snowy for finally ridding the world of that evil monster Drossmire, and a very big well earned thank you goes to all of you for doing such a splendid job. As always, it has been a pleasure for me to enjoy both your company and your expertise, and I know the Gods of the Terrestrial Light are also very happy and wish me to extend to you their extremely grateful thanks.

'What you all need to do now is to go off and enjoy the rest of your holiday! Perhaps we'll meet again another time. You now know wherever you are you are able to reach me. So until then, I again thank all of you, and say goodbye!' and with that he was gone.

'I think we ought to go into Moatcaster and get some lunch now,' Sylvia said, trying to re-focus and get their minds away from the awesome trials and tribulations of the extremely eventful morning.

'You'll have to wait a minute, Mum, until Mary and I have thoroughly examined that storeroom,' David said in rather a serious voice. 'I don't want to go anywhere until we have checked it out. We must be totally sure Drossmire is dead. Only then will we be able to relax.'

At that moment the seven friendly magpies materialized perched on the handrail close to the top of the stairs as the twins reached the top, their spokesman spoke for them.

'Merlin asked us to do any tidying up that might need doing, David, and we are also here to put all your minds at rest. Drossmire is definitely dead and there are no cinders or dust left now for any other family members to use. Enjoy the rest of your holiday!' And they were gone.

Both David and Mary then looked at each other with rather puzzled expressions on their faces, as they both tried to absorb the last bit the magpie had said. After a brief pause for thought, they slowly turned round to descend the steps. Then, having stopped at the same time to face each other, both loudly said, 'What other ruddy family members?'

The End

"MYSTICAL MAGPIES & MYTHOLOGY"

A SERIES OF FOUR SEQUENTIAL STORIES
by
ALAN PRINCIPAL

Four 'crossover' captivating action packed and magical adventures. Exciting family reading suitable for the 'young at heart' from 10 to 100.

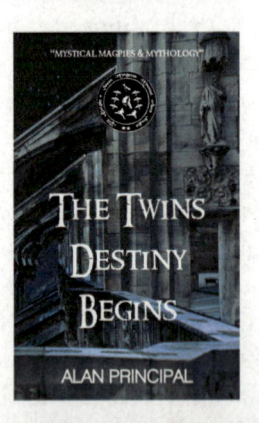

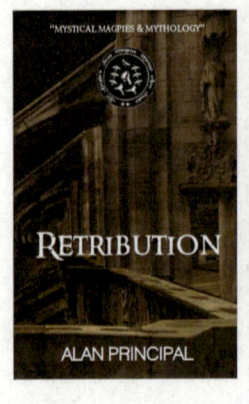

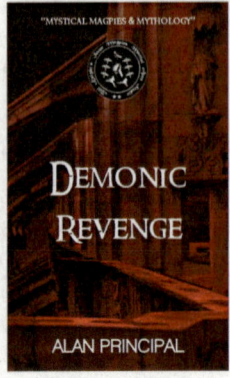

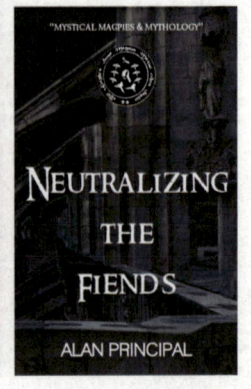